D1176393

BLURB

A secret masquerade hookup leads to complications with Rourke's new boss.

Rourke: As a celebrity personal assistant, I pride myself on professionalism. When a mysterious stranger offers to show me the wonders of a clandestine sex club at the masked ball, I jump at the chance. Because no one will know me, right? One night. No names. No faces. It should have ended there. I had no idea that the handsome, enigmatic man would turn out to be my new employer.

Roman: After the masquerade, I searched for the girl who'd crashed my party, only to find her in my office a few months later. I can't fire her because she's the best assistant I've ever had, but I can't stop wanting her in my bed either.

If you like tension, angst, and a good dose of sexy, then this book is for you.

***This book was formerly released as Sex, Lies, & Lipstick as part of the Bad Boy Billionaire Bachelors Boxset.

THE EXILED PRINCE

SEX, LIES, & LIPSTICK

JEANA E MANN

ISHKADIDDLE PUBLISHING, LLC

CHAPTER 1

ROURKE

$\mathcal{A}$s I stood in the center of Everly's hotel suite, wearing her extra ball gown, her designer shoes, and an expression of shock, I knew this was the granddaddy of bad decisions. Beside me, Everly floated like a graceful princess in vintage Oscar de la Renta, a jeweled tiara on her head, and a delicate silver mask in her grasp. I smoothed my hands over the hundreds of Swarovski crystals sewn to the bodice of my dress and shook my head. My pulse leaped and skittered like leaves scattering in the wind.

"This is not a good idea," I said. The girl staring back at me from the mirror looked like someone else, thanks to a team of professionals, two hours in a makeup chair, and hair extensions. Not in a bad way, just someone different, someone who wasn't me. What would Aunt May think of this transformation? A pang of guilt twisted my insides at the thought of the fairytale evening in front of me while she languished inside the beige walls of a low-income, assisted-living facility.

"Yes, it is. It's the best idea I've ever had." Everly circled me, scouring my appearance with a critical eye.

"Give me one good reason," I said.

"Here." She thrust her phone into my face. The picture of a dark-haired, enigmatic Russian prince stared back at me. My heart skipped a beat. A triumphant smile brightened her face. "Case closed."

"The chances of meeting this guy are less than zero," I grumbled. "You said so yourself."

"Always so negative." Her eyes softened. No one knew the misfortunes of my past better than Everly. "But miracles happen all the time. What if he's your miracle?"

"He's way too complicated for my taste." I waved away her foolishness with a sweep of my hand. "I'm only going because you're forcing me."

She stuck out her tongue and turned her attention back to my transformation. "What do you think, Christian?"

"Excellent." Christian, her stylist, patted his hands over my body in an impersonal way, making me blush, adjusting and tugging on the dress, until he nodded in satisfaction. "Now put on the mask."

I groaned but lifted the white-and-gold filigree mask to cover my face. He clapped his hands together in delight.

"Perfect," Everly said.

"Perfectly crazy," I replied.

For seventeen of my twenty-six years, Everly had been my best friend. She was also the daughter of the former Vice President of the United States, and my boss. We'd attended the same private schools, our lives weaving parallel lines until my parents died and my life had changed. As her personal assistant, I organized the chaos in her life, attended social functions, and kept her company during her travels. Tonight, those duties included crashing London's most exclusive masquerade ball. She had received an invitation. I didn't.

"Stop bitching and be quiet for a second. I need to think."

She tapped a polished fingertip to her lips. "Something's missing, Christian. What is it?"

I studied my reflection but couldn't see anything out of place. My blond hair hung in loose curls over my shoulders, much longer than my normal shoulder-length locks, thanks to hair extensions. Everly's diamond earrings dangled from my earlobes. The ensemble was classy and elegant.

Christian frowned. "It's her lipstick. It's all wrong. She needs a pop of color." He turned to the makeup artist at his elbow and clapped his hands, "Lipstick. Now." In a flurry of panic, she grabbed a plastic case and opened it for his inspection. He shuffled through the dozens of tubes. "No. No. No. Hell no." At last he landed on something worthy of his attention. "Yes. This one."

The girl, pale and anxious, removed my mauve lipstick with a cosmetic wipe and reapplied the new color, a luminescent shade of pink. "This is a test brand. It's not on the market yet." Her anxiety intensified. "I'm not supposed to give it out to anyone."

"Don't be ridiculous." Christian shuffled her aside and scanned me with a critical eye. "Is that better, Everly?"

"Yes!" She hopped up and down. Her voluminous skirt rustled like brittle fall leaves. "You're brilliant, Christian."

"You don't pay me to be average," he said with a cock of his pencil-thin eyebrow.

The makeup artist's shoulders lowered in relief. I tried not to giggle at the absurdity of it all. Fancy, formal events had never been my thing. I preferred a nice, quiet night at home with a good book and a glass of wine.

"Everybody out." Christian clapped his hands together. The others jumped. "Ladies, you are pure perfection. My work here is done. I'll be on my way." He leaned forward and bestowed double air-kisses to Everly's cheeks. Not to me, because I was an employee and therefore no one of consequence. "Enjoy your evening, love."

"Thanks, Christian. You're a doll. Love you." Everly waggled her fingers at him then turned to face me. "The car is waiting downstairs. Are you ready?"

"Tell me again why I'm doing this." Every shred of common sense in my head screamed for me to run in the opposite direction of Everly and her latest zany scheme.

"Because you love me, and I insisted, and I always get my way." Her pretty eyes sparkled. "And because I love you, and I'm worried about you. I want you to have fun and let your hair down for a change. This is my last night as a single woman. We need to celebrate and kick up our heels."

"You don't have to worry about me. I'm fine," I said, more for my benefit than hers.

"Don't lie to me, Rourke. You've been moping around for weeks. Don't think I haven't noticed." She rubbed a hand up and down my back, her forehead crinkling. "I just want you to be as happy as me."

"I am." To hide the truth, I ducked my head and pretended to pluck imaginary lint from the dress. Change scared me. I liked safe and steadfast.

"I can't believe this is our last night together." Her voice trembled.

"I know. I'm really going to miss you."

Reality hit me like a punch in the gut. In a few days, she would be married and fly to Australia with her new husband. I would return to the States to start a new life, one without her in it. The pang of impending loss sliced through my chest. She'd been my rock, and I'd been hers. Although I was excited for her, the selfish part of me wanted to beg her to return home with me. Unfortunately, I had unavoidable obligations just as she did, making our separation necessary.

"You're going to ruin my makeup," she shouted, fanning

her glistening eyes with both hands to keep the tears at bay. I leaned in to give her a hug, but she flinched. "Stop. You'll wrinkle our dresses." Then, going against her warning, she pulled me into a tight hug, crushing me to her. "I love you so much. You know that, right?"

"I love you, too," I said, because I did. I loved her like the sister I never had. She was impetuous, indecisive, and frustrating, but those traits only made her more endearing. "It's going to be great. We're both starting new adventures. We'll Facetime and text. And I'll see you at Christmas." Like always, I felt it was my duty to console her, putting her needs ahead of mine.

"Yes, of course. It'll be amazing." Although her lower lip quivered, she summoned a bright smile and squared her shoulders. "Now, pull your tits up. It's show time."

CHAPTER 2

ROURKE

*I*nvitations to the Masquerade de Marquis were highly sought after and most exclusive. The high-society event provided the chance to rub shoulders with the richest of the rich, the most famous of celebrities, the most notorious of politicians. Everly had earned her invitation by coordinating, with my assistance, a worldwide charity campaign to aid victims of human trafficking. Marrying one of the wealthiest men in the world didn't hurt, either. When her invitation had arrived at our hotel suite last week, she'd been over the moon. Instead of a bachelorette party, she wanted to attend this ball, and recruited me as her partner in crime. The only problem? I didn't have an invitation.

"Isn't this exciting?" Everly chirped. "How can you be so calm?"

"Practice." Beneath my tranquil façade, my insides quaked. The taillights from a long line of expensive cars glowed red in front of us. Bentleys, limousines, exotic sports cars—their sleek fenders gleamed in the approaching twilight. My imagination ran wild at the thought of their occupants. I'd never owned a car, and if I did, it would probably be something normal like a Honda.

"Crap on a cracker! Would you look at that house?" She grabbed my hand and squeezed as our Mercedes limousine rounded a bend in the miles-long driveway and joined the parade of automobiles.

"What have you gotten me into?" I'd been so focused on our last night together that I'd forgotten to worry about the masquerade. As we drew closer to our destination, my knees began to dissolve.

The elegant manor house could have been taken straight from the pages of a Jane Austen novel. Massive columns stretched across three stories of brick façade. Age and history mottled the whitewashed exterior. Our limousine pulled to a pair of mirror-image stairs. Two footmen stepped forward, immaculate in white gloves and gold-trimmed livery, to assist us from the car and up the steps.

"I've changed my mind," I whispered to Everly. With each stride, the steak I'd eaten for dinner threatened to come back up. Why did I let her talk me into these crazy schemes? "I'll wait in the car for you."

"Oh, no." She dug her elbow into my back. "Too late. You're not backing out now."

We entered the house through enormous double doors. Another footman led us through hallways lined with tapestries, portraits, and busts. Outside the ballroom, my heart galloped between my ribs. I placed a hand over my sternum. I'd made it past the front door. No one had asked to see my invitation, the one with the name of Everly's cousin, Beverly Ellis, engraved on it.

"What if I get caught?" I asked, trying not to hyperventilate. Beverly, unable to attend while recovering from appendicitis, shared Everly's penchant for mischief and had willingly turned over the invitation to her cousin for my use. "I don't look anything like Beverly."

"You won't unless you keep acting like an escaped convict. No one uses names here. It's against the rules of the party." Although she smiled and nodded, her tone carried the edge of steel. "Just remember what I told you. Don't take off your mask. Be pleasant but vague. If anyone acts suspicious, make a distraction. Spill a drink on them or pretend to faint."

Despite my worries, I laughed. "Do people really do those things? I thought that only worked on TV."

"I'm serious. If you get into trouble, text me. Remember, the code word is *blowjob*."

"Why do we need a code word? If I'm in trouble, I'll just text that I'm in trouble."

"Where's your sense of adventure? Sometimes you act like you're fifty instead of twenty-six," she said, her expression sobering. "Don't be a middle-aged woman, Rourke. Not tonight. Promise me."

"Someone has to be sensible." At the sight of her wrinkling nose, I gave in. "Fine. I promise."

Taking my elbow, she drew me toward the enormous gilded doors and the liveried footmen waiting to open them. Muffled orchestra music floated through the walls. "There are hundreds of people here. No one is going to worry about one harmless girl. And, if you're lucky, you might get a glimpse of Roman Menshikov."

"I would die," I said, my knees going weak at the thought of our host, the handsome, enigmatic Russian exile. However, he rarely attended his parties, preferring to observe in secret, never mingling.

"Please don't die." She gave my arm a squeeze as the doors parted onto the most decadent display of wealth I'd ever seen.

Men in tuxedos danced with women in elegant gowns,

their faces obscured by masks. Everything sparkled, from the enormous crystal chandeliers to the gilt-framed mirrors and hand-painted details of the architecture.

"Ladies, can I offer you a drink? Champagne? Wine?" A waiter extended a tray of goblets and flutes in front of Everly.

Before we could react, another man came forward, dressed in black from head to toe, his eyes obscured by a simple black mask. He spoke with formal precision in a slight Russian accent. "Good evening, ladies. My name is Ivan, and I am at your service. Before we begin the evening, there are a few items of business we must get out of the way. Will you step this way please?"

My pulse leaped into overdrive. Everly and I exchanged nervous glances. Her eyes warned me to remain calm. My eyes blamed her for talking me into this fiasco. I pressed my sweating palms together and squared my shoulders. We followed Ivan's wide back into a small alcove with a desk. He shut the door behind us. My insides quaked.

"May I see your invitations?" He extended a hand, palm turned upward.

"Of course." Everly's smile belied the trembling of her hand as she drew the heavy cardstock from her purse.

The moisture in my mouth disappeared, taking my voice with it. I hesitated. Everly nudged my elbow. With an apologetic smile, I handed the invitation over to him. He glanced at Everly's but studied mine, his gaze flickering from the card to me and back again. This was it. Would they escort me to the front door, making a spectacle of my shame? My thoughts raced through a dozen unpleasant and humiliating scenarios.

After an interminable span of time, he returned the invitations. "Thank you, ladies." A sigh of relief burned my lungs. I held it back. Circling behind the desk, he withdrew two forms and placed them in front of us, along with expensive gold ink pens. "All guests are required to sign a non-disclosure agreement. Inside the masquerade, real names are forbidden, but you may use any pseudonym of your choosing. Pictures are strictly prohibited. The integrity of this night depends upon your discretion."

"Right," I said. The word came out as a croak. I started to write my name, then realized my mistake and corrected the R to become a B. In a shaky scrawl, I signed Beverly's name. I bit my lower lip and forced a smile. He didn't smile back but took the form without looking at it and placed it inside one of the desk drawers.

"Please make yourself at home tonight. There is a buffet along the far wall and an open bar to the left. You will find the ladies' powder room down the hall behind you and to the right. Should you require fresh air, the terrace is through the doors at the end of the ballroom with steps leading into the gardens. There are many delights to enjoy outside as well. Mr. Menshikov asks only that you do not trespass into his private quarters on the second floor. Should you require anything—anything at all—please do not hesitate to ask."

"Thank you, Ivan," Everly said. "Is Mr. Menshikov here tonight?"

From behind Ivan's back, I mouthed, "What the hell?" She lifted an eyebrow.

"Business has called Mr. Menshikov away this evening. And even if he was here, he chooses not to participate," he said, his expression polite but shuttered. He opened the door. Light and music spilled into the small room. "Please enjoy your evening."

Once he'd left us, I groaned. "That was so close. I thought I was going to pee my pants."

Everly laughed. "Calm down. We're in. Look at this place. Aren't you glad you came?"

"Okay, maybe," I admitted grudgingly now that the rush of adrenalin had receded. "Check back with me in an hour."

"On that note, I'm going to mingle." It was one of the things I loved most about our friendship. We'd never been the type of friends who had to be together every single minute. She patted the glossy strands of her updo. "Do I look okay? Is there lipstick on my teeth?"

"You look fantastic, like you always do." Her personal style, thanks to Christian, hovered on the cutting edge between conservative and classy. With her auburn hair and pale skin offset by the sapphire hue of her gown, she caught the eye of every man in the room. "I wish I had half your beauty."

"Hush. Didn't you see yourself in the mirror?" When I shook my head, she rolled her eyes. "Half the secret to being attractive is self-confidence. You're a hottie, so own it." She put her shoulder against my back and gave a little shove. "Now, tonight, I have an assignment for you. I want you to dance with someone."

"No."

She laughed at my outright refusal. "Come on. I remember the Rourke from college. She was fun and ornery and loved to have a good time. I know she's still inside some-where. Let her out tonight. There are tons of gorgeous men here. Take advantage of the opportunity to meet someone new."

"Fine, but I'm not going to enjoy it." She had no way of knowing that sometimes—when the ache of loneliness grew too massive—I sneaked out of our hotel room and into the bar. A few drinks and a random hookup eased my frustra-tions. I liked the freedom of screwing someone I didn't know. No questions, no commitments, no hurt feelings. The following day, we'd pack our bags and travel to a new destination. I'd leave town with a secret smile on my lips and soreness between my legs, but my heart remained intact.

"I'll check back with you in an hour. Now get out there." She nodded toward the dance floor. "And remember, I'm watching you."

CHAPTER 3

ROURKE

I wandered through the ballroom, mesmerized by the scores of beautiful people. Behind their masks lurked some of the most famous faces in the world. Every now and then, I thought I recognized the curve of a woman's smile or the width of a man's shoulders, but I had no way of knowing who was who. The masks came in all shapes and sizes. Some were elaborate combinations of feathers and gems on a background of satin. Others were sleek and simple like Ivan's. Everly had picked up my mask on one of her many trips to Venice. It rested lightly above my nose, held in place by strings of silk, allowing a clear view of my eyes but obscuring enough to hide my identity.

After a few minutes, I began to grow comfortable among the guests and had to admit I was enjoying the anonymity. Without the threat of disapproval, I could do anything, and be anyone, I wanted.

A brown-haired man in a navy tuxedo tapped my arm. "I was wondering if you'd like to dance?"

Remembering my promise to Everly, I accepted. His aristocratic features and pleasant smile bolstered my resolve to meet someone new. "I might be a little rusty. I haven't danced in years. If you don't mind my clumsy feet, then I don't mind either."

He extended a hand. "It's my pleasure."

I placed my hand in his and let him lead me to the dance floor. The brush of our palms together sent a pleasant ripple along my skin. The orchestra segued smoothly from a foxtrot into a waltz. From the sidelines, Everly nodded approvingly. My heart skipped a beat when he put his arm around my waist. It felt good to be held by a man again. He twirled me around the floor until I was breathless, ignoring the many times I stepped on the toes of his shiny shoes.

At the end of the song, he smiled down at me with full lips and gray bedroom eyes. Beneath the dark blue velvet mask lurked the face of a handsome man, around my age, maybe younger. "That was delightful. You've made my evening."

"Thank you. You're too kind." I smiled. He lifted my hand to his lips, grazing his mouth over my knuckles, sending a shiver of attraction through my body. "You can call me Nicky. And what should I call you?"

Panic evaporated the moisture from my mouth. I cleared my throat. "I thought we weren't supposed to reveal our real names."

"I never said it was my real name." He watched me closely, waiting for my answer, his gaze focused on my lips.

"You can call me—" I searched for an appropriate name. "You can call me Cinderella."

His burst of laughter escalated my panic. "Oh, that's priceless. Well, Cinderella, tell me, how did you come by an invitation to the elusive Masquerade de Marquis?"

I tried to smile and stay calm, deflecting the question with one of my own. If I'd learned anything during my years with Everly, it was that people loved to talk about themselves. "I kind of fell into it." Not exactly a lie but not the truth, either. "What about you? Have you attended to the masquerade before?" I kept walking in the direction of the ladies' powder room, preparing to excuse myself before I got into trouble.

"A few times." He fell into step beside me. "No one turns away an invitation unless they want to offend the host, and Mr. Menshikov doesn't like to be offended." His eyes watched me with the sharpness of a hawk watching a mouse. The predatory nature of his stare raised the tiny hairs on my arms.

"Are you a celebrity?" I kept my tone light and teasing but cast a glance in the direction of the ladies' room, judging the distance.

"In some circles." A dimple popped on his right cheek. "Mostly I'm here because I have friends in high places."

"Are you a friend of Mr. Menshikov?" My sense of self-preservation went to war with my curiosity. I wanted to know more about the enigmatic host without giving too much of myself in return.

"Friends?" The sharpness in his laugh made me flush. Obviously, I'd crossed an invisible boundary. "Roman doesn't have friends."

"Ivan said he's not here tonight." I stopped walking and gave my full attention to Nicky, hoping to coax more information from him. "Do you know him? Roman, I mean?"

"I don't think anyone truly knows Roman." Mystery edged his words. Mistaking my curiosity for the host as interest in him personally, he smiled and took my hand again. He lifted it to look at the ring on my little finger. Delicate strands of silver and gold vines twisted together to form a circle. Amethysts sprinkled throughout the band like tiny flowers. "Your ring—it's very unique."

"It belonged to my mother," I said, running my thumb over it. "My father had it made for her when I was born."

"Ah, how romantic." He stroked the band with a fingertip, the light pressure tickling along my skin. "Speaking of romantic, would you like to take a walk in the garden? There are all kinds of entertainers down there. There's nothing I love more than a moonlight stroll with a beautiful woman." He leaned down, his tone lowering. "Someone said there are naked performers dancing through fire. How can you pass up a chance to see something like that?"

Although his charm was infectious, I shrank away from the opportunity. I didn't want to blow my cover. A few yards away, Everly lifted an eyebrow. Although she didn't speak, I knew her well enough to understand the message. *Get your ass out there. Live a little.*

I squared my shoulders. "Thank you so much for the invitation, but I think I'd like to dance some more." Dancing was safe. With the music swelling and the hum of conversation and laughter surrounding us, there was little opportunity for questions I didn't want to answer.

"Fair enough." He bent low in a deep bow. "May I have the honor of this dance?"

For the next several hours, I danced with Nicky until my feet ached, drank champagne until my head swam, and laughed until my insides quivered. He was delightful, although his prodding questions required my skillful avoidance.

"Who is that man?" I asked, having caught sight of a gentleman near the fireplace, his forearm resting on the mantle. Although I couldn't see his eyes behind his mask, I felt the weight of his relentless gaze following us around the room as we danced. The curling edges of his dark hair hung to his collar, its messiness at odds with the crisp lines of his tuxedo.

"Where?" Nicky followed the incline of my head. "Oh." For the first time, he missed a step. His shoulders tensed beneath my touch, the smile sliding from his face before he recovered. "I'm not sure. He could be anyone."

Was it my imagination, or had I heard a touch of Russian accent in Nicky's reply? "He keeps staring at us."

"Probably because you're so beautiful," Nicky said. In an adept maneuver, he directed us toward the opposite end of the room. Within minutes, I forgot about the stranger, too focused on following Nicky's lead and the heady exhilaration of being held by such a charismatic guy.

"It's getting late, and I have to leave soon," he said, leading me toward the row of chairs along the wall. "I know it's against the rules, but I can't go without learning your name—your real name."

"You know I can't tell you that," I said, still breathless from his touch and the physical exertion.

"But you can. It's just a stupid rule Roman invented for his own amusement. You can tell me. No one has to know." He squeezed my hand tighter, his jaw tightening. "I want to see you again."

"No. You can't." At the flicker of hurt in his eyes, I softened my refusal. After all, he seemed like a nice guy. "There's no point."

"You're married?" His grip loosened on my fingers.

"No, no, nothing like that. It's just that I'm going back to America in a few days." Behind his mask, his eyes searched mine. I fisted my hands, resisting the urge to brush his light brown hair from his forehead.

"I travel to the States frequently. I could look you up. We could have dinner, and you could show me the sights."

"Excuse me, may I cut in?" A smooth, deep voice sliced into our conversation. From his accent, he was American, a New Yorker or somewhere on the east coast.

Nicky and I both turned to face the stranger. A black leather mask prevented me from going further than the curve of full, pouting lips. My gaze traveled from the onyx buttons of his charcoal vest down the perfect crease of his dark gray trousers to the shiny, pointed toes of his black shoes. Unlike the other formally attired guests, the tail of his silver bow tie dangled from the breast pocket of his jacket. The lack of formality seemed out of place and rebellious in a room overflowing with perfection.

"We were having a conversation," Nicky said, his tone acidic. The change in his demeanor caught me by surprise. I glanced from him to the stranger. A palpable air of animosity pulsed between them.

"Watch your manners, Nicky." The stranger's light rebuke reminded me of a parent scolding a rebellious child. "Please forgive him. He's been running with the wolves for too long."

"At least I'm still running." There was no mistaking the competitive edge in his words.

My gaze bounced between the two men. Whatever their relationship, it was complicated and intriguing.

"Not here. Not now. Not in front of our lovely companion." While he spoke, his dark eyes locked onto mine. He took my hand in his long, graceful fingers, his smooth palm gliding against mine, and lifted my knuckles to his mouth. My heart stopped at the brush of his soft lips on my skin. In the background, the introduction to a tango began. "Dance with me."

Three words sent my pulse into overdrive. "The tango used to be my favorite, but I haven't done it in years." I panicked at the thought of the intricate moves.

"Don't worry. I'll take care of everything." After another kiss to my knuckles, he led me to the center of the dance floor. The guests parted, making way for us, their eyes heavy on my back. I couldn't blame their stares. This man exuded confidence, elegance, and power. He placed my left hand on his waist and took the right in his palm. Shying away from his gaze, I stared at his throat. The top two buttons of his crisp white shirt gaped open, revealing a triangle of smooth, tanned skin dusted with black hair. He squeezed my hand, demanding my attention. "Eyes to mine. Don't look at your feet. Follow my lead."

Behind the mask, his eyes were dark, almost black. Anxiety closed my throat. This would either be an amazing experience or extremely embarrassing. Probably the latter. The music swelled, and we began. Within a few steps, I captured his rhythm. He was strong and forceful, moving me into each position, twirling me out then snapping me back against his chest. I gasped at the press of my breasts against hard muscles.

"Very nice," he said. A neatly trimmed beard and moustache couldn't obscure a square jaw, reminding me of a jaunty pirate.

"Thank you." The warmth of his approval spread through my chest.

"I'm going to have to step up my game." His eyes glittered with challenge.

"Yes. You are." They were bold words for a girl who hadn't danced the tango in six years, but I didn't care. I liked the feel of his body against mine and the strength in his arms. More than anything, I enjoyed the way his overpowering maleness made me feel feminine and dainty.

"Be careful what you ask for." His arms tightened around me. I slid slowly down his torso and pressed my breasts into the hard lines of his body. When my eyes reached the level of his narrow hips, he yanked me to my feet. The crowd gasped.

"You surprise me," he said.

"You aren't the only one with secrets, sir." The hem of my skirt swirled around my ankles. The slit opened to flash a stretch of my leg and the white garter belt around my thigh. I felt his gaze go there. It returned to mine, flashing with desire.

"So, I see." By the humor in his tone, my answer pleased him. Or maybe it was the garter. There was no more time for conversation as the intensity of the music continued to escalate.

This was more than a dance. It was a test. A game of dominance and submission underscored by sexual tension. I stiffened my arms and pulled away. The words of my dance instructor floated through my subconscious. *Be angry. Let the audience see the struggle.* He snapped my body to his and stroked a leisurely hand from my armpit to my hip. Goosebumps peppered my skin. I spun away, only to be returned by a tug of his arm. We continued our war of wills around the room.

At the finale, he bent me backward over his thigh, arching my spine until the ends of my hair swept the floor. The smooth fabric of his trousers rubbed against my bare back. I was totally at his mercy, one foot on the polished marble, the other lifted to keep from tumbling over. His lips grazed the column of my throat in an erotic caress. Excitement and lust simmered in my veins. I was living my fantasies in the arms of an exotic stranger.

The music ended, and the crowd erupted into applause. I'd been so engrossed in our power play that I'd failed to notice the onlookers, or that all the other participants had moved to the sidelines. We were the only couple on the dance floor. Under normal circumstances, this kind of attention would have made my stomach queasy, but beside him, it seemed natural.

Adrenalin buzzed through my head, more intoxicating than the liquor. He eased me to my feet. Once I'd steadied myself, he released my hand and bowed. "Thank you for the dance." Before I could respond, he melted into the crowd. I watched his broad shoulders disappear. A curious sense of regret tempered my euphoria. That was it? One amazing dance, and he left?

Someone touched my elbow. I erased the disappointment from my expression and turned to find Everly. She drew me aside and fanned her cheeks with a cocktail napkin. "Holy crap, Rourke. That was hot. Who is that man?"

"I'm not sure." I stared wistfully in the direction he'd gone, but my attention wavered at the weight of Nicky's disapproving stare on the stranger's backside. What was it between those two men? "I think he's Roman Menshikov."

Everly's gaze followed mine in the direction the stranger had gone. Her brows lowered. "It could be, but I don't think so. Everyone says he's out of the country."

"I know, but there's something about him." I searched through the guests, looking for disheveled black hair and an unshaven jaw.

"Did you ask him?"

"How could I? I certainly can't tell him who I am. Ivan will throw me out."

"True. Well, no matter. You have another admirer," Everly said, her eyes dancing with delight, nodding toward Nicky. "This is so exciting. Are you having a good time?"

"Yes." The answer required no conscious thought. "I haven't had this much fun in years." As always, my thoughts returned to her welfare. "What about you?"

"I'm having a great time. A few of my friends are here." She squeezed my hand. "Thank you so much for coming. I could never have attended on my own. This is the best bachelorette night ever."

"You're welcome. Thank you for dragging me here." I smiled back at her, thrilled by her excitement.

"I think you should hook up with one of those men." The

mischievous glint returned to her eyes. "A good lay would do wonders for your self-confidence."

"Oh, no." I shook my head.

"Yes. You absolutely should. Think about it. Everyone here is anonymous. It's like Las Vegas. What happens here, stays here." Her eyebrows lifted, but she quickly got her expression under control and ducked her head. "Don't look now, but the brown-haired gentleman is coming this way, and he doesn't seem happy." She waggled her eyebrows. "Look at you, stirring the shit. I'm out of here. Have fun and be safe."

"Don't you dare leave me, Everly." Despite my plea, she sashayed toward the back hall, waving her fingers over her shoulder in my direction. "Traitor." I steeled myself for more of Nicky's questions.

"Did you enjoy your dance?" he asked. If he was displeased with me, the face beneath his mask gave no indication of his feelings. Neither did his tone. "You were a vision out there. I don't think I've ever seen anyone quite so breathtaking."

"Thank you." I felt the blush creeping into my cheeks. "I'd like to take the credit, but my partner was responsible for most of it."

His jaw flexed, a small but obvious indication of his disapproval. "He always had a flare for the dramatic."

"I thought you didn't know each other." Something about his demeanor had changed since we'd parted earlier.

"We knew each other as children, but we haven't run in the same circles for a very long time." As if he sensed my mistrust, he shook his head and smiled sheepishly. "I apologize if my behavior is unacceptable. I'm afraid the sight of you in another man's arms has brought out my jealous side." A lot of years had passed since any man had flattered me quite so thoroughly and with such skill. However, pretty words had never turned my head.

The orchestra segued into the next song, an upbeat, modern tune. Over Nicky's shoulders, I caught sight of the mystery man. He was talking to a busty beauty with raven hair. The plume of her elaborate gold mask jerked and bobbed as she spoke. His words might have been for her, but his eyes were mine. A dozen yards separated us, but the heat of his gaze seared into me.

"I'm sorry, what did you say?" Too late, I realized Nicky had asked me a question.

His gaze followed mine. A frown of frustration shaded his smooth features, a frown he quickly erased. "I said my schedule is full next week, but the week after, I'll be in Manhattan for meetings. I'd love to take you to dinner."

"I appreciate the invitation, but it's just not possible." Once I returned home, I needed to find an apartment and a job and check in on my aunt. Nervous anxiety squeezed my stomach. I didn't want to think about real life. Not yet. Not until I had no other choice.

Across the room, the dark stranger ended his conversation with the busty woman and strode toward us like a shark slicing through a school of fish. The crowd parted for him then closed in his wake. A wave of heat swept up my chest and into my neck before settling in my face.

"Tell me your name. Please." Nicky took my hand, drawing my attention back to him. "I'm begging you."

"Don't beg, Nicky. It's embarrassing," the stranger said.

I placed a hand on my stomach to steady my breathing as his cologne reached my nose. The spicy, masculine, and hypnotic scent conjured images of tangled limbs and fingers clutched in bedsheets.

Nicky turned and said something low and guttural in Russian to the stranger. Although my Russian was rusty, I caught a few snippets of profanity and the phrase *don't mess with me*.

The stranger laughed before turning to me. "I apologize. We're being rude."

"Are you speaking Russian?" I asked. "I'm afraid I don't understand much."

"Just as well. It's an uncivilized language," the stranger said. His stern smile signaled the end of the topic. "I'm about to go for a walk. Would you like to accompany me?"

Nicky touched my elbow. "Don't fall for his pretty words. You can't trust him."

"Walk away, Nicky," the man said. From behind the edges of his plain black mask, dark eyes glittered dangerously.

"No, I don't think so." The younger man squared his shoulders.

"I'm not asking."

Nicky sighed, his tone turning petulant. "You're breaking the rules."

"Ah, but you forget. I make the rules." The stranger's posture straightened, his height growing. The cut of his tuxedo suggested a powerful chest beneath his tailored lapels.

"Did you ever happen to think that maybe she's not interested?" Nicky's voice teemed with irritation.

"And maybe she is. Did *you* ever think of that?" the stranger asked.

"Gentleman, please stop talking about me like I'm not in the room," I said, finding my voice at last. Both men had the good grace to look abashed.

"Again, I apologize," said the stranger, his eyes locking with mine. Something about this dark man lit a fire in my veins. I wanted to know more. Who was he? Why was he here? What had he done to gain an invitation?

"I'd love a tour," I said. "Nicky and I were about to say goodnight anyway."

"Can I have a word in private?" Nicky ducked his head to my ear, speaking too low for the stranger to hear. "Are you sure about this? He's not the kind of man to be trifled with. You might find yourself in over your head."

"I appreciate your concern, but I can take care of myself."

Nicky glared at the stranger, a silent conversation passing between them. Then his gaze turned to me. After an awkward pause, he let go of my hand and bowed. "It's been a pleasure, Cinderella. I hope our paths cross again soon."

"Goodnight," I replied. "Thank you for your company this evening." With long strides, he crossed the ballroom and disappeared into the hallway. Part of me was sad to see him go, but the other part felt relief. Nothing could come of our relationship. It was best to end things before it became too messy. As much as I liked Nicky, I preferred the company of the dark man at my elbow. His attention made me uneasy and exhilarated, like those precious moments of anticipation before a rollercoaster plunged over the first hill.

"Cinderella? Interesting choice of names." He closed the distance between us until his shiny shoes rested next to my sandals.

"Yes. I like it. And you are?" *Dangerous.* The answer flashed through my head. I pushed away the assumption. Nothing about this man seemed threatening, except to my ovaries, which had begun a dance of excitement.

"My friends say I'm the devil." Once again, he took my hand in his. The intimate glide of his fingers between mine unleashed a repressed longing to feel those fingers elsewhere on my body. "But I suppose if you're Cinderella, then I'll be your Prince Charming."

"That's a little presumptuous, isn't it?" I baited him in an uncharacteristically flirtatious tone, my confidence buoyed by Nicky's attentions and too much champagne.

"It's not presumptuous. It's a truth. That's something you should know about me. I only deal with facts."

Somehow, in the space of our conversation, we'd drifted toward one of the curtained alcoves along the perimeter of the room. When the curtain closed behind us with a whisper of velvet, and the bright colors of the ballroom dimmed into candlelit darkness, I realized I was alone with a man I didn't know. A very tall, ominous man, whose broad shoulders and penetrating stare dwarfed the room. Nicky's words echoed back to me. *He's not the kind of man to be trifled with.* I swallowed a frisson of fear, as intoxicating as it was disturbing. No need to freak out. The party continued outside the alcove. Help was only a few feet away.

"I thought we were going for a walk." My gaze flicked to the heavy drapes, judging the distance in case I should need a hasty escape.

"Later. First, I want to know more about you." His hooded gaze traveled over my face, lingering for two heartbeats on my lips. How many nights had I dreamed of a man like this—one who'd thrill and frighten me? He braced a hand on the wall by my head, hemming me in. Up close, he smelled of leather, expensive cologne, and fine, rare things.

"There isn't much to tell really," I said, my knees weakening. Although his nearness set my senses on high alert, I didn't feel threatened, just aroused.

"You're an American?"

"Yes, a New Yorker." I bit my lower lip to keep from giving away more than I wanted.

"Why did you come to this party?" He leaned closer, edging me backward until the hard paneling chilled my backside.

"Why does anyone come to these parties?" I asked, feeling lightheaded at his closeness.

"To enjoy anonymity in a safe and nonjudgmental atmosphere. To experience decadence without the threat of discovery."

"You sound like a travel magazine." I pressed my palms against the wall at my sides and reveled in the escalation of my pulse.

"People come from all over the world for this experience. There are places here—secret places—with access given to only a select few. I can take you there. We can explore those mysteries together." He drew in a deep breath, angling his head and scenting me. The primitive gesture caused an immediate pulse in my sex. "You haven't answered my question."

"Yes," I said, feeling weak-kneed, excited, and frightened in rapid succession. "To all those things. I want to experience all of that."

"Let me show you everything your heart desires." The low, seductive music of his voice and an excess of champagne dulled my common sense. I had the distinct feeling I was being seduced by Satan, and the safety of my soul hovered in the balance. "Well, Cinderella, will you join me?"

"Okay." For a second, I thought he was going to kiss me. When he increased the distance between us, lowering his hand from the wall, disappointment washed over me.

"Before we begin, may I see your invitation?"

His request sent my stomach plummeting to the floor. "No, you may not." I lifted my chin, trying to pull together my faculties. "I don't have it on me. It's with my friend."

"You're not a very good liar. And you're not Beverly." Each of his words raised my temperature another degree until I thought my insides would combust. How would he know Beverly unless he was Menshikov?

"I never said I was Beverly." If I was caught, I had nothing to lose by bluffing. Meeting his gaze, I conjured a playful smile. So many sins could be hidden with a smile. "I came here under the assurance that no one would question my identity. If anyone found out that I was here, it could be very —damaging—to my reputation and my career." This was total bullshit, but I kept going, even though my heart jackhammered against my ribs. "Are you threatening my privacy? Because I'm pretty certain that's a direct violation of the rules."

"Rules were made to be broken." Full lips rolled together. I couldn't help staring at the gesture and wondering how those lips tasted, how they kissed. Would he be forceful? Gentle? Would his hand fist in my hair while his knee parted my thighs?

"I'd bet my life that you don't have an invitation." His eyelids lowered to slits. "I know everyone at this party. Everyone but you."

"Are you sure? I'm sure we've met before. In Rome? Or maybe Paris?" I met his gaze, refusing to blink. "I think we're done here," I said, calling his bluff. "If you'll excuse me."

"God, a woman with balls. I love it." He threw back his head and laughed. The deep sound shimmered over me, easing the tension in my shoulders. "I'm one hundred percent certain we've never met. I couldn't forget someone as lovely as you." The weight of his gaze crawled over my face, lips, breasts and hips, scraping over my nerve endings, alighting my body with a new and intriguing kind of fire. He rested a fingertip under my chin, tilting my eyes up to his, the tip of his thumb grazing my skin. "Very well, Cinderella. You win. I'll give you a pass this time."

"I'll stay, but only if you behave." God, he was handsome. The silk mask and thick but well-groomed beard couldn't hide the sharp lines of his square jaw, the chiseled planes of high cheekbones, and the knife-blade edge of his nose.

"I realize I'm out of line, but you've piqued my curiosity." If only I could see his eyes. Were they blue or brown? Under the shelter of his mask, I couldn't tell.

"Are you Menshikov?" How else could he know that I entered the party under the guise of Beverly Ellis?

He studied my eyes for a long second. "No, I'm not. But I know him very well."

"Are you going to tell him?"

"That you're here without an invitation?"

Too late, I realized my mistake. "No, I mean—"

He silenced my words with a fingertip to my lips. "Hush. Your secret is safe with me." His gaze dipped to my mouth again. I slid my tongue across my bottom lip, suddenly famished and thirsty, dying for relief from a hunger I never knew I possessed. "For a price."

CHAPTER 4

ROMAN

*E*very spring, I hosted the event of the year, not for myself but for the amusement of my friends. I'd grown bored with the whole thing years ago and rarely attended. A capable set of planners managed the entertainment and catering. The guest list, however, remained my sole responsibility. I culled the names of interesting people from the media and my personal acquaintance. The mix of personalities and backgrounds provided an entertaining atmosphere. Over the past decade, the Masquerade de Marquis had become notorious for decadence and debauchery, all committed under the guise of secrecy.

From the library window on the second floor, I watched the guests filter into the house and mentally crossed their names from the invitation list. A Saudi prince and his security team arrived in a caravan of black limousines. The senator from Wyoming came alone in a rented Jaguar. An entire boy band tumbled from the seats of a passenger van, cocktails in hand. Although I didn't care for their music, I did enjoy their zest for life and success.

"Can I get you anything, sir?" Ivan asked, appearing from thin air in the doorway.

I jumped. "Jesus, Ivan. Can't you knock first?"

"I did, sir." His smirk, however, suggested a smug satisfaction in catching me mid-daydream. "I thought you would like to know. The guests are arriving."

"Yes, I can see that." I returned my attention to the window. My gaze snagged on a vision of loveliness wearing a white jeweled gown. Long blond hair tumbled over her shoulders. A white mask highlighted delicate features, a pert nose, and small pointed chin. "Who's that girl? The blonde?"

He joined me at the window and gazed down at the pair traveling up the steps on the arms of two footmen. "I'm not sure. Would you like me to ask?"

I watched her disappear, graceful and uncertain, through the enormous double doors. "No. Someone that beautiful doesn't need an invitation. Just keep an eye on her, would you? Make sure she's not a reporter."

"She's lovely, isn't she?" Ivan studied me, trying to discern my motives. Nosy bastard.

"Aren't they all?" I shrugged and schooled my features into disinterest.

"Would you like me to bring her up here?" A sardonic smile twisted his lips. "Female companionship might do your —er—um—temperament some good."

"What are you trying to say, Ivan? That I've been an uptight asshole?"

"Not at all. Just trying to anticipate your needs, sir." He stared down his nose at me in his imperious manner, completely unapologetic.

"No. You can go." I unrolled my shirtsleeves, carefully keeping my face turned from him. "I'll be in my office."

"As you wish, sir." He bowed and left the room on silent

feet. Even after a lifetime together, he still called me "sir" and treated me like the royalty I'd once been, despite my requests to the contrary.

Inside the dark, shadowy confines of my office, I switched on the security monitors and watched the mysterious blonde negotiate the ballroom. It took a lot of balls to crash this party. Many had tried, most of them reporters or paparazzi, in search of a scoop. I studied her posture and mannerisms and decided she was harmless enough, until Nikolay arrived at her side.

Like a true hunter, he'd sniffed out the prettiest female and attached himself in record time. We'd been in competition our entire lives, or rather, he'd been in competition with me, for the best business deals, the fastest cars, the prettiest girls. It was the last one that caused the most strife. We had similar tastes in women. We both liked voluptuous blondes. And, as fate would have it, my ex-fiancée had been both.

I pressed the call button on the phone. "Greta, bring my tuxedo to my office, the charcoal one."

"Yes, sir. Right away," she replied.

Ten minutes later, I entered the ballroom through a secret panel in one of the alcoves and melted into the throng of guests. I maneuvered through the bodies until I was near enough to smell the mystery girl's perfume—a heady combination of lavender and spices and soap. God, she was even more intoxicating up close. Full breasts, narrow waist, round hips and an ass carved from the hands of Botticelli.

I had no intention of meeting her, but I could tell by the tilt of Nicky's head, his possessive hand on the small of her back, that he was interested in more than her company. And I just couldn't have that. Tales of intrigue and revenge peppered my family history, and I was no exception. He'd done me wrong, and this was my chance to even the score.

Yes, I understood the pettiness of my grudge, but I was rich and bored, and I loved nothing more than a good challenge. Something he knew better than anyone.

CHAPTER 5

ROURKE

*W*hen I lifted my gaze, I found the stranger staring at me, eyelids hooded, lips pursed. The breadth of his chest rose and fell with a deep breath. The appearance of this raven-haired mystery man rekindled the desires I'd fought to curb. Sensuality oozed from his pores. I stared into his turbulent eyes and longed to run my fingers along the line of his beard, to place kisses on his mouth. Did the taste of wine linger on his tongue?

I pressed both palms against the wall. My inner voice screamed, *Leave now. Run while you can. Nothing good can come from this.* But I was tired of lonely nights and long days of work. I deserved a night of fun and sin. After all, it was only one night. Tomorrow, I'd return to the monotony of reality, quiet nights at home with a book, occasional museum visits, and solitude. Tonight, I wanted to live.

"I'll pay the price," I whispered.

"Are you sure?"

"Yes. I'm sure."

His hand traced the neckline of my dress, drifted over the swell of my breast, along my ribs, and came to rest at my hip.

I wasn't a fool or an innocent; there was no mistaking that the price would be personal and intimate. *Please, God, let it be personal and intimate.* A small smile played on his mouth. He extended a hand, palm up. My natural response was to take it. His smile broadened. "Shall we go for a walk then?"

"What about the price?"

"First we play. Then you pay." He let the gravity of his statement settle. I got the feeling he was waiting for me to bolt.

Instead, I smiled and met his eyes. "I can hardly wait."

We began our tour with an exploration of the gardens. Torches lit the meandering walkways. Their flames cast dancing shadows over the foliage. The beat of tribal drums reverberated inside my chest. The sound grew louder with each step. At the first clearing, an enormous bonfire glowed. Its heat burned my cheeks. Naked men and women, covered in neon paint, swayed and writhed to the rhythm. I watched, fascinated, with Prince Charming close at my side.

"They're performing an ancient Druid rite," he said. The red-gold firelight sharpened his profile. I tried not to stare at him, but my body thrummed from his proximity. "The nudity is a bit of artistic license, but it works, don't you think?"

"It's breathtaking."

My answer seemed to please him. His lips curled at the corners. In the darkness, his eyes remained hidden, but I had the feeling they'd reveal nothing. "More?" he asked.

"Yes, please."

Taking my hand, he placed it in the crook of his elbow and led me down the next pathway. On the outside, I fought to appear calm, but my insides whirled in a tempest of conflicting emotions. What was he thinking? Who was he? Was he Roman Menshikov, despite his earlier denial?

Cowardice prevented me from asking again. I didn't want to push him away, not yet. Not until I had to leave.

"Are you in London for long?" he asked after a span of silence.

"A few more days," I replied. "And you?" A warm breeze carried the scents of earth and smoke and jasmine. Our feet crunched on the packed gravel.

"I'm only here for a short layover before flying home."

"And where is home?"

"I have houses all over the world." His enigmatic reply fueled my curiosity.

"That's not an answer."

"I spend a lot of time in New York City. I have offices there and a penthouse. It's a good base, halfway between London and California. It's as close as I've ever come to a real home." The forthright answer caught me off guard. I hadn't expected a reply and certainly not a detailed one, one I could sympathize with. "Your turn. Have you always lived in New York?"

"No. I moved there when I was fourteen to live with my aunt. My parents died within a few months of each other, and she was kind enough to take me in until I finished high school." For a brief moment, I forgot that he was a stranger and that I was trespassing at a party to which I didn't belong. His easy demeanor and keen interest had almost tricked me into confessing my secrets. I bit my lower lip.

"I'm so sorry for your loss." He halted and brushed my hair over my shoulder. The graze of his fingertips against the bare skin of my back sent a shiver through my body. "I understand what it's like to lose your parents. I lost mine when I was very young. It makes a hole in your heart that never quite heals."

I sucked in an audible breath at hearing my own words thrown back at me, words I'd said so many times. "Yes, I know. You're still functioning, but a piece of you is missing and always will be."

"And your aunt—she was very kind to take you in." Wind and music filled the air, muffling our voices. I nodded. "Were you happy with her?" His dark head bent lower to capture my words.

"Oh, yes. Very happy. She's a wonderful person." Suppressed tears stung the backs of my eyelids. I blinked them into submission. I didn't want to talk about my aunt or the illness threatening to take her from me. "What about you? Were you happy?"

"One of my father's friends took me in. He raised me as his own when he didn't have to. I have no complaints." We'd come to a fork in the path. He gestured to the intersection. "Which way shall we go? Left or right?"

"Which do you suggest?" The left path arched toward a copse of trees. The right path angled down toward the lake.

"Well, to the right is beauty and tranquility and a sight worthy of Monet or Pissarro. To the left is something just as beautiful but much more interesting and very wicked."

My breathing stuttered. The choice wasn't a choice at all, but a given. "Left, please."

"Are you sure?" One of his thick black eyebrows arched.

"Yes. No. Well, now I'm not sure. Why is it wicked?"

One corner of his mouth curled upward like a comma, like he knew a secret, a very dirty secret. "The price for what lies down that path might be higher than you want to pay."

"Can I pay in installments?" My answer was intended to be tongue in cheek, but Prince Charming cocked his head, considering, face somber.

"That's an excellent idea." His gaze dipped to my mouth. He ran his tongue over his lower lip. I mimicked the action, suddenly famished for a taste of him. "I suppose you owe me a kiss for the fire dancers then. Your first installment."

He took a step toward me. One of his hands went around my waist and yanked my hips against his. The forceful, unexpected move stole my breath and made my pulse pound. The buttons of his vest bit into my sternum. Lower down, I felt the press of his stirring cock against my stomach. His free hand tangled in the hair at the nape of my neck and angled my mouth to align with his. My lips parted, eager to make contact with his warm mouth.

"What are you waiting for?" I asked when three interminable heartbeats passed.

"For you to give your consent." His voice had turned husky, growing deeper and richer.

"I consent."

The instant those words floated into the air, he closed the gap between us and pressed his lips to mine. The delicious scent of his cologne filled my nose. I placed my palms on his chest. Beneath the linen of his shirt, hard muscles tensed. This—this was what I'd been yearning for. The tip of his tongue eased between my teeth. Slow, probing sweeps of my mouth devastated my inhibitions. His fingers tightened in my hair. I could fall into a kiss like this and never come up for air.

Too soon, he eased back, leaving me panting and dizzy.

"Jesus," he muttered. "I wasn't prepared for that."

"Me neither." My lips buzzed. He held me for a second longer then pushed me away with a gentle hand. Yearning for more, I swayed toward him.

"Easy, Cinderella." The look of shuttered interest returned to his expression. "This is only the first installment, and I have a feeling there will be many, many more."

The promise in his voice made my stomach flip. "I hope so."

"Are you having a good time?"

"I'm having an excellent time, thank you." Lightness of

spirit buoyed my footsteps as we continued our journey. For the first time in a few years, I had no responsibilities, no one to worry about but myself, and I'd just kissed the most interesting man I'd ever met.

"I'm glad to hear it." He kissed the back of my hand. This time, instead of letting go, he threaded his fingers through mine.

We passed through a grove of aged trees, their branches thick with foliage, their shadows vibrating from the torchlight. On the other side, the crenelated top of an ancient tower came into view. I pointed, forgetting my manners, feeling like a child in Wonderland. "Look. A castle."

"It's called The Devil's Playground," he said. "The original castle was built here in the twelfth century. It has a very brutal history. Only the keep is still standing. The rest fell down, and the stones were robbed to build the manor house."

"Can we go inside?" I asked. As a kid, I'd daydreamed about castles and knights in shining armor. The weather-beaten stones, the moat, and arrow slits brought back all those fantasies.

"If you wish." From behind his mask, his eyes searched mine. "But I have to warn you, it's not what you're expecting. I'm afraid it might shock you."

The headiness of his kiss, the warm breeze, and the surreal surroundings erased my inhibitions. I wanted to test the boundaries that had ruled my life for the past twenty-six years. Tonight, there were no rules, no repercussions, no expectations. Anonymity had given me a gift, and I intended to use it to the fullest.

CHAPTER 6

ROURKE

*P*rince Charming slid a key card through a slot at the enormous door. It beeped, and the tiny light turned green. We stepped into a stone chamber lit by lanterns. Their dancing flames lit the walls with an eerie red glow.

"This would have been the original entrance. See the murder holes above and the arrow slits across from us? Anyone storming the castle would have been skewered by arrows and burned by boiling oil or water thrown down from overhead." He opened a second set of doors and motioned for me to step into the next room. "Only special guests are allowed in here. There's an application process and approval to gain access."

"There are people in here?" All I heard was the whistle of the wind against the window panes and the faint thump of music in the distance. "Is this, like, a club?"

"Not 'like' a club. It *is* a club. Admission is one million dollars per person. But tonight, you're my guest." He swept an arm to our left. "This way. Watch your step."

My high heels tapped on the uneven stone floor. Warm

fingers held my elbow, guiding me up a circular staircase to the second floor. We entered a narrow passageway, barely wide enough for the two of us. Wood paneling covered the walls.

His breath tickled my ear as he bent to speak. "It's not too late. We can still leave if you want."

A small chandelier lit the room. The golden light cast a warm glow on his bronzed skin.

I placed a palm against the wall. The more he protested, the greater my curiosity grew. "No. I want to see."

"Alright, but I warned you." Was it my imagination, or did his tone hold a kernel of amusement?

His shoulder brushed mine. The accidental contact simmered along my arm. The narrow space heightened my awareness of him—his breathing, his leather-and-citrus scent, the strength of his body beneath that perfect tuxedo. With his eyes glued to my face, he slid open a panel on the wall.

"The lord of the castle used to spy on his guests through this opening," he said. "While they dined and enjoyed his hospitality, he listened in on their conversations." I lifted to my tiptoes, straining for a look. He raised an eyebrow then kicked a small stepstool in front of me.

At first, I saw nothing but a spacious room, wood paneling, tapestries, and the glint of armor. Logs popped and cracked within a fireplace opening taller than me. I cast a quizzical glance at my companion. He nodded to the tiny window, his expression inviting me to return.

On my second look, two leather sofas came into view. A woman, wearing nothing but a mask, bent over the back of the first sofa. Behind her, a muscular young man pounded into her. His trousers puddled around his ankles. The sound of flesh smacking flesh filled my ears. My mouth dropped open. I wanted to look away, but I couldn't stop staring at the flex of his buttocks as he thrusted or the bounce of the woman's tits from the impact. In the corner, two men kissed. At their feet, a pair of women performed oral sex on them.

"You're shocked," said the stranger.

"Yes. I—I had no idea." Words seemed inadequate to describe my conflicting emotions. Part of me was horrified and embarrassed, but the other part—the baser, animalistic part—was turned on by the display.

"Do you want to go?" The rawness in his voice scraped over my eardrums. "Or do you like it? Do you want more?"

"More." The dry walls of my throat constricted. "Show me more."

CHAPTER 7

ROURKE

*W*hen I was nineteen, I'd lost my virginity to Vance, a graduate student at Everly's university. He'd been patient and gentle. Although the initial experience had been awkward, the subsequent encounter had awakened a sexuality I hadn't realized I possessed. We'd arranged to meet once a week until the end of the year. He'd taught me a lot about sex but nothing about love. And I'd been fine with that. After the unexpected deaths of my parents, I didn't want to need anyone.

I turned back to the naughty, filthy scene through the peephole. A new kind of desire unfurled within me. One that had always been there but had been squelched, denied, and ignored. Nice girls didn't enjoy scenes like this. But then, I wasn't a nice girl.

"Once again, you've surprised me, Cinderella," said the stranger. He stood close behind me to peer over my shoulder. The muscular front of his chest pressed into my back. Each of his words brought a puff of warm breath on my earlobe and sent a shiver down my spine, the good kind, the kind only a man with a smooth bass voice provided.

"Does this happen often?" I asked, my voice strained and unfamiliar. "I mean, do people always come here for this?"

"The keep is only open by invitation and only at the masquerade." The buttons of his tuxedo bit into my back, and so did something else lower down, something long and thick and promising. "But The Devil's Playground is a very elite, very secretive club. There are a handful of other locations around the world."

"Do you always watch, or do you participate?"

"Sometimes I watch. Sometimes I participate."

The thought of him touching another woman, fucking her in that room, filled my veins with jealousy. It also turned me on. "How does one become a member of this club?"

"By referral only. There's an extensive application process and several interviews to vet the members. Why? Do you want to join?"

"I don't think I could afford it." I sucked in a breath to ask another question, but a new couple entered the great hall, bringing us to silence. It was the woman he'd been talking to earlier, the one with large breasts and raven hair. She glided over the handwoven rugs. The elegant man at her side gripped her hand tightly, possessively. He led her to a strange bench, one with restraints on both ends. They kissed, long and lingering. The intimacy of the act made my body ache in deep, dark places, and I wished someone would kiss me like that. Forgetting the man at my back, I lifted a hand to cup my breast. The sharp point of my nipple jutted through the thin fabric, hard against my palm.

The man drew down the zipper of the woman's dress. It whispered into a pool of organza at her feet. She stood nude in front of everyone, her eyes locked with her companion's. They paid little attention to the others, too engrossed in their own pleasure. If only I could be so shameless, so proud of my body. I pressed closer to the window and strained for more.

He bent her over the velvet-upholstered bench, binding her hands and legs with the leather restraints at each end. The woman rolled her hips into the bench, visibly impatient, while the man undid his fly and pulled out his impressive cock. No wonder she was anxious. I licked my lips when the man feathered his fingertips along the woman's spine, his touch delicate and worshipful. No man had ever touched me that way, and according to the direction my life was going, they never would. Not unless I made a change.

The pair began a sinful ceremony of desire. Music filtered into the room through hidden speakers, loud and hedonistic, with a thumping bass that shook the walls. More people entered the room, some watching openly, others participating in their own scenes. All the while, my heartrate accelerated, and the ache between my legs grew.

"You like this." His smooth voice murmured in my ear, a new roughness to his speech. "You like to watch."

"Yes. I do." Revelation dawned in a combination of shame and excitement. I had no idea how long we'd been standing in front of the narrow peephole. It could have been minutes or hours, but I couldn't look away.

"It's nothing to be embarrassed about." His lips brushed against the curve of my neck. Gooseflesh raced along my shoulders. "Do you like to be watched?"

"I'm not sure. I've never done anything like that before." My heart ricocheted between my ribs and my sternum. Was he going to ask me to join the others? Did I want to participate? My thoughts tumbled and scattered like dry leaves in a tempest.

He offered a hand to help me down from the step stool. My knees quaked. For a second, the room shivered and tilted before I regained my balance. We stood facing each other. My backside mourned the loss of his body heat.

"Would you like to be watched with me?" The question

exploded in my head, stealing my breath and creating dampness in my panties. "Or would you like for me to watch you with someone else? Speak your wish, Cinderella, and I can make it come true."

"I'm not sure if I'm ready for the grand hall." The thought of stripping in front of the others made my stomach queasy. "Not down there. Not with them."

"If you want to experiment, this is the best place to do it. You're safe here. No one will ever know. No one but you and me." His words flowed over me, seductive and beckoning. "And we're strangers. Tomorrow, we'll be different people, living different lives, separate lives."

Hooded eyes searched mine. I had no idea what color they were, except they were dark and brooding and boiling with lust. He crowded me against the wall. The smooth paneling felt cool against the skin bared by the V in the back of my dress.

"Tell me, princess. What do you want?"

I placed a hand on his chest. The muscles beneath my palm flexed. In this moment, he was raw and powerful and everything I'd ever dreamed of having in a lover. "I want to end the ache between my legs. I want to feel naughty and needed and free." While I spoke, his hand smoothed over my shoulder, down my ribs to stop at my hip. His dark head bent to nibble along the tendon between my jaw and shoulder. "I want to be with you."

"All you had to do was ask."

For a brief interlude, his hand left my body. The wall gave way behind me. His arm slid around my waist to keep me from falling. The front of my body pressed against his hard chest. He walked me backward, his strong thigh between my softer ones, into a dimly lit, windowless room with shadowy corners. The tempo of the music gained speed. My pulse clambered to keep up with it. Once my eyes adjusted, I could make out the shapes of furniture and austere portraits on the paneled walls.

"Are you afraid?" he asked, his voice deeper and rougher than before.

"No. Should I be?" My own voice quavered the tiniest bit, not with fear but with the excitement of shedding my old skin and becoming someone new, someone adventurous and dangerous.

"I would never hurt you. Not in a bad way. Not unless you asked me to."

My behind met the edge of a sofa. I curled my fingers into the plush velour covering. Questions fizzed in my brain like bubbles in champagne. What had I gotten myself into? Should I ask him to stop? No, I didn't want this to end. I needed more.

His hands smoothed over the curve of my hips and down my legs. He gathered the hem of my dress and slid it up to reveal the filmy white triangle of my panties. My pulse escalated. This was absurd. I was about to have sex with a man I'd known for less than a few hours. Actually, I didn't know him at all. He could be anyone: a prince, a criminal, a—

"Unzip my pants." The terse command came from lips poised at the curve of my jaw and ended my thoughts. His breath scalded my skin in hot puffs. I ran a palm along the length of his zipper in exploration and found an impressive rod of steel behind the gabardine, thick and long. The zipper growled as I lowered it. Silk boxers peeked through the opened V of his trousers.

"You like to be in control," I said.

"Always." He pressed the first kiss to my throat and dragged his lips along the tendon running to my shoulder. "Nothing turns me on like obedience."

I shivered and swallowed around the lump in my throat, one born of anticipation. "Are people watching us?"

His throaty chuckle reverberated against my skin, erupting in tiny explosions of desire along my synapses. "Maybe. Maybe not. It's entirely possible. All the walls in this fortress have eyes."

The thought of someone watching us set fire to my lust. Would the unknown spectators touch themselves while spying? Would they feel the same heat and lust I'd felt watching the others in the great room? I rolled my hips against his. The unending desire in my core required release, and soon.

"You're my fantasies come to life," he muttered, more to himself than to me. I liked this facet of my stranger. The threads of his self-control began to fray. I felt it in his hands, his lips, the hardness of his cock. "What should I do with you, my lovely?"

"Use me," I said and let my head tip back to bare my throat.

The second kiss landed at the notch in my collarbone. One of his fingers traced the lace edge of my panties then slipped behind the barrier to stroke my folds. I moaned at the unexpected trespass. "Do you like that, Cinderella?"

"Yes." My heart was beating so hard and so fast, I thought it might leap out of my chest. One of his fingers slipped inside me and curled upward while his thumb circled the tiny bundle of nerves at the apex of my sex. The man had skilled fingers, but then, everything about him screamed of culture and expertise and knowledge. He knew the exact amount of pressure and the proper speed to bring me to a fever pitch within minutes. At the brink of orgasm, his fingers withdrew. I groaned in protest.

"Easy, princess. Just putting on our insurance policy." He withdrew a foil packet from his pocket, ripped the covering, and quickly sheathed his cock in the condom.

Too many things happened in concert for my head to

wrap around. He stepped between my legs, grabbed my knees, and tipped me backward. I gasped, certain I'd tumble over the other side. I spiraled into information overload—the luxurious scent of his cologne, the grip of his hands, the fabric of his pants against my inner thighs. It was all too much, yet not enough. I still needed more.

The crown of his cock nudged my center. In one rough thrust, he was inside me. The delicious burning bordered on painful. He was too big and too long for me to take at once, so he withdrew a few inches then wiggled his hips until he was seated to the root. The deliberate truth of the act satisfied my deepest fantasies. This was what I'd longed for on all those cold winter New York nights.

"Hold on," he said against my mouth. "I won't be gentle."

I gripped the couch to keep from falling. He pounded into me, ruthless and unheeding. It was brutal and punishing, and just what I needed. The impersonal intimacy of the act suited me. There would be no hurt feelings or awkwardness at the end. Knowing this gave me the freedom to enjoy every second.

When his hands moved to my hips, I clutched his shoulders. Somewhere to my left, I heard the slide of wood, the muffled intake of breath from someone other than the stranger. My orgasm rushed over me with unexpected violence. I stifled a scream, choosing to bite my lower lip instead. The flutter of my walls around his cock spurred him to double his speed. He rocked into me with selfish abandon, milking my orgasm to fuel his own. At last, he stiffened and spilled into the condom between us.

Throwing back his head, he growled, the sound furious and triumphant. "Fuck, yes. Yes."

As the rush of endorphins receded, shock muddled my thoughts. Had I really just fucked a stranger in some secret room on Mr. Darcy's estate? I wasn't sure if I was dreaming or insane. It had happened so fast. I didn't even know this guy's real name. Before, back in the hotel, I'd have laughed out loud at the idea, but now—God, I gloried in it.

"That was amazing. Perfect," he murmured, his lips against my ear. "You're a dream come true, Cinderella. Thank you."

"You're welcome?" The response came out as a question, because I wasn't sure why he was thanking me. Surely a man of his extreme good looks and magnetic personality had his pick of women. Another, bigger part of me, felt smug and satiated. Slowly, the fog receded from my brain. Everly was going to love this story, but I couldn't tell her. It was too personal, too perfect to be shared with anyone.

He continued to praise me in broken phrases. "So tight... slick...pretty."

We were still connected, his cock inside me, my dress pushed up to my waist. A series of aftershocks caused my walls to clench around him. He waited for the last flutter to recede then, with a small sigh of contentment, withdrew. I watched, my eyelids heavy, as he removed the condom and disposed of it. After tucking himself away, he helped me to my feet and smoothed my gown over my hips. I hesitated, feeling lost, wondering if I should go, uncertain if my legs would carry me to the door.

Everly's impeccable timing saved me from the unknown. The buzz of her incoming text vibrated the silence. The stranger arched an eyebrow but didn't comment. I dug through my clutch for my phone with trembling hands. In my haste, the contents spilled onto the floor. I grabbed the phone to cease the vibration and shoved everything else back into the purse.

Everly: *Where are you?*
Everly: *Are you okay?*
Everly: *The car is here. Are you ready to leave?*

The stranger leaned over my shoulder and whispered in my ear. "Don't go. Stay with me."

"I can't." As much as I longed to spend the night in his arms, there was no point. He had his life to live, and I had mine. This ended now.

"I can have my car drive you home later." His gaze stroked over my body, stoking the fire of need in my belly. "I'll take you to breakfast in Paris."

"You have no idea how tempting that sounds, but I really can't."

He pursed his lips. "I suppose it would be out of line to ask for your real name." I shook my head. "You know, I could find out your identity with a few phone calls."

"Please don't."

We stared at each for a long time. The magic of the night dissipated with each passing moment. At last, he nodded. "Another time then. It's been a pleasure, Cinderella."

I ran down the path to the manor house, my thighs slick with arousal and my pussy aching. Everly met me at the front steps, a worried frown on her face. "Where have you been? I've been looking all over for you."

"It's a long story," I said. But once we were in the car, safely on our way home, I couldn't bring myself to tell her. I could scarcely believe it myself. Instead, I tucked the truth away to savor in the quiet moments between waking and dreaming and never spoke of it again.

CHAPTER 8

ROURKE

*E*verly's wedding went off without a hitch. After many hugs and tearful goodbyes, she flew to the other side of the world to begin her life as a married woman, and I returned to New York City. The next three months passed in a blur. With the approaching end of the lease on Everly's Manhattan apartment, I started packing my things and fought against the heavy weight of sadness. My footsteps echoed around the empty rooms. In her absence, I floundered in my efforts to create a new life.

I'd lived with her since the age of nineteen, so I'd had no idea how expensive real estate was in the city. Rent for the smallest efficiency apartment was way above my means. Unless my next employer had live-in accommodations, I'd have to consider moving to the suburbs, enduring a longer commute, or living in a place the size of a postage stamp. In addition to the costs of moving, I had the additional financial burden of full-time care for my aunt to consider. Her welfare superseded my personal needs, and I'd do whatever necessary to keep her happy and comfortable, even if that meant living in the projects.

"You're welcome to stay with me until you get on your feet," Mena said at our luncheon one day. She'd been Everly's publicist for the past year. We'd worked closely during that time and continued to have lunch in Manhattan once or twice a week.

"I still have a week left on the lease." The sidewalk outside the café teemed with people hustling along the sidewalk, on their way to jobs, to loved ones, to friends. I envied their sense of purpose. With a smile, I forced a note of positivity into my voice. "Something will come up."

"Of course. Things always have a way of working out." Although her tone was soothing, reproach hovered in her eyes. "What about Winchester? He made you a nice offer. Maybe he's still looking."

Everly had given me six months' advance warning, but I'd been too busy planning her wedding and tying up her loose ends to purse a job until now. I'd passed up two offers, thinking more opportunities would present themselves. Several had seemed promising but had required relocation from New York City, and I couldn't leave my aunt. "No. I already checked. He hired someone last week."

She patted my hand. "You can always do temp work for me, running errands, odds and ends. I know it isn't ideal, but the offer is there if you need it."

"If something doesn't come up soon, I may take you up on it." Although I smiled on the outside, inside I cringed with self-recrimination. Why, why, why had I gotten myself into this predicament? I should have made the job search a priority. "I appreciate the offer."

Sunlight caught the auburn streaks in her short brown hair as she gathered her laptop and purse. "Jiminy, I'm late for a consultation." A frown creased the pale skin of her forehead. "You know, I wasn't going to say anything, but my friend knows someone who's looking for a personal assistant for her boss in Manhattan. I told her you probably weren't interested."

"Really?" My spirits perked. I sat up straighter. "Why would you say that?"

"The guy is a real asshole. I mean, he's gone through eleven assistants in the past year." Her long fingers scraped through her hair, giving it the perfect touch of messiness. "The pay and the perks are off the charts if you can deal with his lack of personality."

"Oh." I slid down in the chair. Although I needed employment, I didn't want to take a job that wouldn't suit me. I also didn't want to wait until my funds dried up or Aunt May was evicted from the nursing home. "It might pay the bills until I find something else."

"True." The contents of her smart red purse jangled as she dug through its depths. "I've got her card here somewhere. Where is that thing?" At last, she smiled triumphantly. "Here it is."

I turned the small black card over in my hand. The front held two words in delicate silver print. "Blue Sapphire," I said aloud. On the back was a woman's name and email address. "What's Blue Sapphire?"

"As in Blue Sapphire Cosmetics? Blue Sapphire Records? Blue Sapphire Airlines? Blue Sapphire Railways?" She rolled her eyes. "Seriously, Rourke, sometimes I wonder if you lived under a rock most of your life. But I know that's not true, because you've been traveling the world with Everly."

Automatically, my gaze drifted to the billboard on the opposite side of the street, high above the traffic and midday bustle. A scantily clad model reclined on a velvet sofa, one arm draped across the back. The gold plume of her black silk mask sent an immediate shiver down my spine, transporting me back to the Masquerade de Marquis. Across the bottom of the billboard, the slogan read, "Indulge in luxury. Indulge in Blue Sapphire Cosmetics."

Mena shouldered the strap of her purse and pushed her chair beneath the table. The legs screeched over the tile floor. "Crap. I've got to run. Just email your info to that address, and I'll tell my friend to put in a good word for you."

※

*W*hen I got back to the apartment, I typed out an email to Julie Baker of Blue Sapphire and attached my resume and letters of reference from Everly and her father. After that, I had nothing to do but wait for a response to the dozens of resumes I'd already sent out. It wasn't like I could go door to door in search of employment. My type of work hinged on referrals, word of mouth, and a high-priced headhunter.

Two days passed. I finished boxing up my things and made arrangements to stay with Mena in Brooklyn for a few weeks. Between job searches, I browsed the internet. When that grew too mind-numbing to continue, I did the one thing I'd vowed never to do—I ran a search on Roman Menshikov. Although three months had passed, I still thought about the tryst at the masquerade when I couldn't sleep, under the cover of darkness. My palms perspired as I scanned through the hits. For a man of his status and infamy, he had a surprisingly small web presence. No Twitter account. No Instagram, Facebook, or Snapchat. There were, however, a few pictures from society blogs and scandal rags.

I clicked on the first picture of Roman as keynote speaker at a business luncheon. He was tall, broad-shouldered, and dressed in a tailored black suit. The enlarged photograph revealed chiseled features and full lips. I studied his face, looking for similarities between this man and my Prince Charming. Since leaving the masquerade, I'd begun to think of him as *my* prince when I touched myself in the lonely, late night hours. Prince Charming had collar-length hair, wavy and black, and a thick, neat beard on his jaw. Roman Menshikov was clean-shaven and had close-cropped hair, but his coloring was the same. They could be the same person or not. It was too hard to tell. Part of me wanted this enigmatic dark prince to be *my* prince, and part of me wanted him to remain anonymous, mysterious, and unreachable.

My phone rang. I jumped like I'd been caught spying and giggled at the absurdity. The phone number was unfamiliar. I answered anyway, thinking it might be an interview request. "Hello? This is Rourke Donahue."

"Hello. Ms. Donahue. This is Julie Baker with Blue Sapphire Group. How are you this evening?" A husky female voice spoke in a smooth southern drawl, North Carolina maybe, or Virginia.

"I'm fine, thank you. How are you?" Meanwhile, my head stumbled to wrap around the caller's identity. Blue Sapphire? I glanced at the clock. Seven o'clock on a Sunday evening. I hadn't expected a response at this hour on a weekend, or at all for that matter.

"I'm sorry for calling so late, but I received your resume, and your qualifications are quite impressive. We'd like to offer you the job." She paused, waiting for my response. "Can you start tomorrow?"

"You want to hire me? We haven't even met yet." I pressed a hand to my stomach, hoping to calm the swarm of butter-flies inside.

"Given Everly Martin's glowing recommendation and a letter from the former Vice President, an interview is unnecessary." Her pause allowed my brain to catch up with the information. "We're really eager to have you on our team."

"I—I—I need salary details and benefit information before I can make a decision," I stammered.

"Of course. I just sent an email with the employment contract and all the information. I think you'll find the salary more than generous." As she spoke, the email notification popped up in the right corner of my computer screen. I gaped at the six-figure salary, full health benefit package, clothing allowance, living expenses, six weeks of vacation, and bonus structure. "And, of course, you'll be given an apartment suite for the length of your employment."

If I hadn't been sitting down, I'd have fallen over. I blinked rapidly, certain my eyes had failed me. "Is this for real?"

For the first time, her professional façade broke, and she laughed. "Yes. It's absolutely true. Blue Sapphire pays its employees very well. The company also expects a lot in return. You'll be on call twenty-four hours a day, seven days a week, unless you're on vacation. And the job can be quite... demanding...at times." In retrospect, her pauses around the word *demanding*, combined with Mena's warning, should have sent up red flags. The money and perks, however, dazzled my mind. I pursed my lips, thinking. An offer this late on a Sunday evening, sans interview, reeked of desperation.

"This is a respectable offer, but I'm afraid my salary requirements are a little higher." I held my breath, hoping she'd take the bait. "I'll need at least another five hundred per week."

"Um, well, okay. I'll adjust the contract, and we can go over it tomorrow." Her rapid response meant I should have demanded more money. Either way, the sum was still way above what Everly had paid me.

"What time should I be there in the morning?" I asked, the decision made. If the job turned out to be intolerable, I could always quit.

"Excellent." Did I hear relief in her tone? "I'll email the address and details. Check in at the front desk by eight AM."

CHAPTER 9

ROURKE

*A*fter a fitful sleep, I awoke with a sore throat and headache. My summer allergies had flared into a frenzy. Fan-freaking-tastic. Due to puffy eyes, I had to wear my glasses instead of contact lenses. The seams of my favorite suit groaned, and the buttons of my skirt threatened to pop off when I tried to force them through the button-holes. All those croissants and cappuccinos with whipped cream had finally caught up to me. I had to settle for an outdated pantsuit that made my butt look flat and my thighs chunky. Gazing at my reflection, I couldn't help comparing the girl from the Masquerade de Marquis to this fright. The hair extensions had been removed the day after Everly's wedding, and the sunny highlights had faded to dark blond. No matter. It would have to do. Christian was back in the city. Once I received the clothing allowance, I'd get him to pick out a more suitable wardrobe.

Julie Baker met me at the reception desk of the Park Place address. She was nothing like I'd imagined. Medium height, smooth brown hair coiled into a low chignon, late thirties. A worried frown added age to her features, but she managed a cool smile and hustled me toward a private elevator. "You'll need to wear the security badge at all times. The badge will give you access to all of Mr. Menshikov's private areas."

The bottom dropped out of my stomach. I placed a hand on the wall to keep from keeling over. "Mr. Menshikov?" I managed to croak. "Roman Menshikov?"

"Yes. Is that a problem?" She studied me intently.

"No, no, of course not. I'm just surprised." I stared straight ahead and cursed the flare of heat in my face. The elevator seemed to rocket toward the top floor, our final destination. After a deep, calming breath, I tried to soothe my anxieties. Prince Charming wasn't Roman Menshikov. There might have been a passing resemblance, but the online photographs had been proof. So why did I have this insistent case of panic? What if I was wrong? What if it was him? I couldn't possibly work for someone I'd screwed, let alone under such notorious circumstances.

"Mr. Menshikov has eight professional assistants. You'll be assisting him directly in his personal affairs, coordinating his private schedule with his business calendar, running errands, and aiding him in general with whatever personal needs he requires." She rattled through a dozen other things, most of which my shocked brain failed to capture.

Too soon, the elevator reached the top and opened into a vestibule. We stepped directly into the foyer of the apartment. To my left, water splashed down a granite wall, into a koi pond. Bright light spilled from the glass ceiling two stories above. Straight ahead was a huge winding staircase, and beyond that the walls of the apartment were floor-to-ceiling windows overlooking the New York City skyline. She led me to the living room. I sat on a black suede sofa and spent the next hour signing paperwork, including a twenty-page non-disclosure agreement. Afterward, she handed me a set of key cards and security codes.

"There are six floors. The bottom three floors house the security team and apartments for staff. The kitchen, dining room, living room, and sitting room are on this floor. There's a library, home theater, gym, pool, and bedrooms on the floors above us."

I lagged behind, entranced by the cool-charcoal-and-gray furnishings, the colorful Picasso hanging over the sofa, and the opulence of details. Understated elegance characterized every piece of furniture. Priceless artwork and sculptures punctuated the open spaces, their loveliness displayed by well-placed lamps, chandeliers, and recessed lighting. An annoyed glance over Julie's shoulder reminded me to pick up the pace. I trotted to keep up with her rapid strides.

"Mr. Menshikov usually has breakfast in his study on the fourth floor. You'll want to meet him there each morning with coffee, his personal mail, and to go over his schedule before he heads to work. You'll also need to scan the news headlines for anything of note. He's especially interested in political unrest." The rapid-fire instructions swam in my head. "Make sure his dry cleaning has been delivered from the previous day and that his wardrobe is coordinated for any meetings he might have. I'll introduce you to the household staff later."

We wove through a formal dining room, a sitting room, and a series of closed doors. With each passing step, my mouth became drier. What if the man on the other side of those enormous double doors was Prince Charming? How would I handle the situation? Julie rapped on one of the doors. I wiped my sweaty palms over the hem of my jacket.

"Mr. Menshikov? May we come in?"

"Enter," said a terse, deep, male voice.

Julie opened the door and motioned for me to wait at the threshold. A man stood on the far side of the study, speaking guttural German into a Bluetooth headset. One hand was shoved into the pocket of his elegant trousers, pulling the fabric taut over a hard, muscular ass. I held my breath, waiting for him to face us.

"Jesus, where have you been?" He ended his call and turned.

Nothing about his face seemed familiar. His hair was short and styled with gel. The skin of his lean, square jaw was shaved smooth, his nose less straight and longer than the picture in my head. I tried to compare his face to my memory of Prince Charming but came up short. It had been three long months since that night. The mental image of my prince had faded with time. I had a general impression of his physical appearance, but the intangible things like his heated touch, the taste of his tongue, and his scent stayed with me.

"We're right on time," she replied calmly.

Then he saw me. "Who the fuck is this? Where's Mary?"

Mortification blazed up my neck.

"Her name was Marsha, and she quit. So did Rene, Enya, and Sheldon," Julie said. I admired the way she lifted her chin and held her ground in the face of his intimidating posture. He ignored her and strode to his desk. The easy grace of his body as he slid into the high-backed leather chair spoke of power and authority and a man who worked out every day. "This is Rourke Donahue. She's your new assistant."

"Why didn't you tell me?" A grimace of displeasure marred the chiseled planes of his face.

"I did, sir. Last night."

Manicured fingertips drummed on the desk. He shook his head, eyes trained on a stack of printed papers. "Well, there isn't much to be done about it now, I suppose. You'll take care of this, I assume? I don't have time to train another one."

"She comes well recommended. She worked for Everly McElroy Martin," Julie said. I marveled at how easily she handled his gruff demeanor. "Former Vice President McElroy gave her a glowing recommendation." I warmed at the memory of Everly's father and his kind words for my service to his daughter.

Was it my imagination, or did Roman's shoulders tense beneath the straight line of his suit? I didn't have time to analyze the blip in his cool façade before he turned his gaze on me. Not on me, but *at* me. Because his eyes never met mine—not once.

"Coffee," he said.

"I'm fine. Thank you," I replied.

"Not you." He shoved a ceramic mug into my hands with the words "World's Greatest Dad" across the front. "Me."

Julie gestured to the wet bar a few yards away. Open doors revealed glass shelves filled with decanters, crystal glasses, a mini-fridge, and coffee machine.

"Cream or sugar?" I trotted to the coffee machine and poured rich, dark liquid from the glass carafe. The aroma wafted up to my nose.

"Black." His sigh of exasperation traveled down to my toes. This had to be the most unpleasant person I'd ever met. At least he was hot. I returned with the coffee and placed the handle in his outstretched hand. He nodded. "Sit."

After a glance at Julie for confirmation, I perched on the edge of the uncomfortable metal-and-glass chair across from his desk. Whoever this man was, he wasn't Prince Charming. He couldn't be; I wouldn't allow it. Steel-blue eyes stared at the computer screen mounted beneath the glass surface of his desk. His lips, while full, pressed into a hard line. A full minute passed before he spoke again. "I need you in here by six-thirty each morning. You'll have coffee ready, my full itinerary, and any urgent messages. Afterward, you'll ride with me to my office. Put your number in my contacts." He slid his phone across the desk. I caught it before it fell over the edge. "Under Speed Dial 11. Is your passport valid?"

"Yes." The walls of my throat scratched over the single word. At his frown, I hastily typed my digits into his contact list and handed the phone back.

He slid it into the inside breast pocket of his suit jacket. "I travel frequently, and I'll need you with me." His gaze went to my neck and scraped over my outfit. I tugged on the straining buttons of the jacket. Heat burned in my cheeks. "Have you moved in yet?"

"Not yet. I haven't—" I stopped midsentence when he waved his hand through the air.

"Julie, send movers or whatever she needs. Get her in here today." With a flick of long, elegant fingers, he shut down the computer. He stood and tugged down his white cuffs beneath the sleeves of his black jacket. Everything about him was crisp and clean and sharp-edged. "Make sure she has computer access and the passwords to my email accounts before tomorrow."

"Yes, Mr. Menshikov," Julie said. She followed him to the door.

He paused at the threshold and spoke over his shoulder without turning around. "And take her shopping, would you?"

I watched his broad back disappear into the hallway and blinked, feeling like I'd been run over by a dump truck. The door slammed behind him.

Julie smiled weakly. "He comes off a lot harsher than he really is."

"Really?" I mused dryly. "Because 'harsh' isn't what I'd call it."

For the first time since we'd met, a genuine smile cracked her features. "You'll get used to him. I promise. Most of the time, he's tolerable. He's been going through some challenges lately, and it's made him grumpier than usual." She exhaled, like she was releasing the tension from her body, and gestured toward the door. "You heard Mr. Menshikov. Let's get you settled in your apartment." Julie led me down the hallway to a second elevator, talking as we walked. "There are eight bedrooms and eleven bathrooms. Your suite of rooms is on the fourth floor." She opened the door into the foyer, clasped her hands behind her back, and waited for my response.

I stood on the marble floor and gaped. Everything was done in tones of cream, taupe, and blush. Crown moldings and plush carpeting stretched as far as the eye could see. I felt like I'd stepped into an article of *Architectural Digest*. This had to be a mistake. "I'm staying here?" I pointed to the room. "In this place? Just me?"

"Yes. Just you." After an amused shake of her head, she moved further into the apartment. "It's small, but there are two bedrooms, two and a half baths, a galley kitchen and dining room. The maid will come in once a day. You can put your laundry outside the door."

"I can do those things for myself."

"It's a perk of the job. I suggest you use it. You're going to be too busy for mundane chores, and when you do finally get some downtime, the last thing you're going to want is to wash clothes."

CHAPTER 10

ROURKE

*T*he rest of the day passed in a whirlwind. While I went over the details of Roman's schedule with Julie, movers brought my things to the new apartment. By the time I finished the day, they'd unpacked everything. My clothing hung on velvet hangers in the walk-in closet, and my toiletries had been carefully placed in the bathroom drawers.

I wandered around the place, awestruck and overwhelmed, feeling like I'd landed in someone else's life. In the kitchen, the shelves of the cabinets and refrigerator overflowed with staples. Fresh bedsheets and towels filled the linen closets. Every detail of my needs had been addressed, from paper towels and napkins down to toilet paper and tampons.

After a long soak in the elegant tub, I flopped onto the bed and tried to calm my whirling thoughts. Exhaustion weighted my eyelids. I was almost asleep when my cell phone rang. I answered groggily. "Hello?"

"Rourke?" Everly's voice brought me to a sitting position. "You sound funny."

"I've got a sore throat. Allergies are kicking my butt," I said. "What about you? How's vacation in Tahiti?"

"It's amazing, like my husband. We're having the best time." The joy in her tone brought a smile to my lips. Hearing her happiness made the pain of separation more bearable. "What about you? Someone from Blue Sapphire Group called to get a reference on you. Did you get the job? Have you seen Roman Menshikov?"

"Um, good, yes, and yes." I lowered my voice. "I'm sitting in one of his apartments right now."

"No way! Get out," Everly shrieked. "Is he the mysterious stranger from the masquerade?"

"I thought he might be, and there is a resemblance, but I don't think so. This guy's a total ass." In detail, I enumerated the many discrepancies between the two men. I fell onto my back and stared at the coffered ceiling. "He never even made eye contact with me. Not once."

"Oh, Rourke, I'm so sorry."

"It's okay. I'm fine. Everything is fine," I said, stumbling to soothe her misgivings while shoving aside my own. "This is a great opportunity. One year with this guy, and I'll have my pick of jobs. The money is great, and this apartment is unbelievable. I'm sending pictures."

"Well, maybe it won't be so bad then." Her voice caught on the last word. "I really miss you."

"I miss you too." The backs of my eyelids stung. If we continued down this line of conversation, we'd both dissolve into tears, so I changed the subject. "How's married life?"

We talked for an hour. She filled me in on the details of life on the opposite side of the globe. I let her talk, enjoying her chatter. The sound of her voice felt like home. After the call ended, however, I felt lonelier than ever. I laid on the bed and stared at the ceiling. Somewhere, above me, Roman Menshikov was sleeping.

CHAPTER 11

ROMAN

For the past week, I'd been fighting a headache. When I woke up on Tuesday morning, I felt like my skull might split in two. The last thing I wanted to do was spend the day in meetings and arguments with a team of legal piranhas over the custody of my daughter. Claudette, my ex, wanted full custody with an exorbitant amount of child support. To punish me, she'd taken Milada out of the country.

Ivan rapped on the door of my bedroom. "Sir, are you awake?"

"Yes, I'm up." Which was only a partial lie. My feet were on the floor but my ass remained firmly planted on the bed. "Bring me some aspirin, would you?"

He opened the door, silver tray in hand. Two white tablets and a glass of water balanced on the center. As always, he'd anticipated my needs before I did. I shot him a look of gratitude, swallowed the medicine, and gulped the entire glass of water.

"You should drink more water," he said, staring down his crooked nose with intense dark eyes. "And less vodka."

"I don't remember asking for your opinion." I sauntered toward the shower. Each step sent a knife blade of pain through the center of my brain.

"And I don't remember asking if you wanted it," he replied dryly.

Following a quick shower and shave, I grabbed a random suit from the enormous closet and got dressed. Ivan stood in front of the window, hands clasped behind his back, and stared at the gray dawn. Whatever went on inside his mind eluded me. He'd watched over me since childhood, but I didn't begin to understand him.

"And how are you this morning, Ivan?" I joined him at the window and threaded silver cufflinks into the sleeves of my white shirt.

"There he is—my bundle of sunshine." Ivan's eyes crinkled at the corners in a rare show of humor. I had no idea how old he was. He could have been anywhere between fifty and seventy.

"What's on the agenda for today?" Usually my assistant would go over the schedule with me, but I had yet to find a reliable one. There had been so many that I'd given up learning their names a long time ago. Now I had another new one, a girl who'd probably prove more of a nuisance than a help. "Have we heard back from Claudette's attorneys?"

"No. They haven't responded to your offer yet. I expect we should hear something this afternoon." His expression remained neutral, his voice even. In all our years together, I'd never heard him raise his voice. We continued to stare across the awakening New York skyline.

"What about the other thing?" I asked.

"What other thing?" A smirk teased his mouth. I put up with his wisecracks and teasing because most of the time, I deserved it.

"You know what other thing." Since the masquerade, the mysterious woman had hovered in my subconscious. She'd been the perfect mixture of innocence and vixen. My cock thickened at the thought of her, the pert nose, the bee-stung lips, and the dimpled chin. No one had interested me since then. Although I'd promised not to pursue her, it didn't mean I couldn't investigate her background. I thirsted to know the tiniest details—where did she sleep, who were her friends, her likes and dislikes.

"Ah, yes. Your Cinderella." The smirk on his swarthy face blossomed into a full-blown grin, a rarity for him. "What about her?"

"Stop fucking with me, Ivan. Did you find her or not?"

"I found her a month ago," he said, his amusement continuing to grow.

"Why didn't you tell me?" The impertinence of this man never failed to amaze me. While others cowered at the sight of me, Ivan treated me like the unruly child I'd once been.

"You never asked." He spoke the truth. Negotiations with Claudette, business meetings, and worries over Milada had eroded my precious time.

I lifted an eyebrow. "And?"

"She's not for you," he said simply.

"What's that supposed to mean?"

"It means she's a good person, a normal person, and not part of your world of debauchery and decadence."

We stared at each other. He knew all my secrets, all my weaknesses and sins, and stood by me in spite of them. "Everyone has a price, Ivan. You know that."

"I do." He clasped his hands behind his back and returned his gaze to the window.

"So, find her price." With an irritated sniff, I clipped the silver tie bar onto my shirt.

"Like I said, she's not for you," he repeated, signaling the end of the conversation. "However, I've lined up four potential women for your approval later this week." The weight of his gaze landed on my face. It was my turn to hide my thoughts. "I'm sure one of them will be to your liking."

"I don't need to like her," I snapped, feeling ridiculous and out of sorts. I was used to having my way and didn't like being denied. The absurdity of my lifestyle grated on my nerves. What kind of man needed someone to obtain his sex partners? Yet, it was a necessary evil. The need for release itched beneath my skin, a never-ending, relentless discomfort born from too many lonely nights. Unfortunately for me, only one woman fulfilled my fantasies, the one woman I couldn't have.

Ivan didn't reply, just arched a thick Russian eyebrow at my outburst, the same way he'd done when I was ten and hadn't gotten the pony I'd asked for.

"I'm sorry." Regret appeared as quickly as my temper had. I clapped a hand on his shoulder and turned toward the door. "I appreciate your help. Thank you."

❦

I made the trek to my study, reveling in the silence of the apartment. With all the chaos inside my head, I craved peace and quiet. The situation with Claudette weighed heavily on my thoughts. I hadn't spoken to my daughter in almost a month. With every passing day, I died a little inside. She was the only light in the darkness of my life. I had no idea where she was or how she was doing, if she missed me, if she wondered why I hadn't come to see her.

The new girl greeted me with a smile and a cup of coffee in her outstretched hand. I gave her a cursory glance—ill-fitting suit, sensible shoes, dark blond hair in an uptight bun.

No matter. Looks could be altered with money and effort. As long as she did a passable job, I could learn to live with the rest.

"Good morning, Mr. Menshikov," she said, in a broken, croaky voice. The office lights reflected off the thick lenses of her glasses.

"Morning." I took the coffee and stared at it. Black and steaming hot, the way I preferred. It seemed like a small thing, but the last few assistants hadn't been able to grasp the concept.

"I wasn't exactly sure what you needed from me this morning. Julie had a previous commitment, so I went over your appointment book. It looks like you have four conference calls and three meetings on the schedule. Do I need to call and confirm any of them or would you like me to reschedule anything?"

"No." After a beat, I took my chair behind the desk. My computer was already powered on and ready to roll.

"I ran through the news headlines for this morning and printed out a few topics of interest." She pointed to a half dozen sheets of paper. I skimmed the topics. This girl was good.

"Next time, you can send these to my phone instead of wasting paper." I tucked the sheets into my portfolio for later. Meanwhile, the pressure between my temples continued to escalate.

"Do you need anything else?"

"No." Everything on my desk had been straightened and arranged, still in coherent piles, but neat and orderly. "That will be all, Renee." I dropped my gaze to the computer screen, already engrossed by a flood of incoming emails. Her light footfalls treaded toward the door then paused. When she didn't leave, I glanced up. "Is there something else?"

"My name—it's Rourke."

"Right." I returned my attention to the computer screen. "That will be all."

CHAPTER 12

ROURKE

I closed the office door and stepped directly into the path of a solid man in a black suit. His arms gripped my biceps to keep me from banging my forehead on his chest.

"Ms. Donahue, pardon me." The Russian accent laced a familiar voice. "Are you okay?"

Panic ignited in my chest and raced up my neck. I hadn't expected him to be here. "Yes. I'm fine." Following a deep breath, I retreated a step to put space between us. Meanwhile, adrenalin sent my pulse into overdrive. What if he recognized me? I should have come forward about the masquerade in the interview. Then again, there was no interview, and therefore, no chance to confess. At this late date, there was no graceful way to bring up the topic.

"I am Ivan Petoskey, Mr. Menshikov's chief security officer." He engulfed my small hand with his large, square one. Anxiety twisted my insides. If he recognized me, he didn't let on.

"Nice to meet you." To my credit, the words came out confident and calm, the exact opposite of how I felt.

"I am happy we ran into each other. I need to speak with you for a moment, if I may." His request prodded my heart from a trot into a gallop.

"I was just on my way to meet Julie." I glanced at my watch, eager to escape his prying eyes. The less time we spent together, the better. The less opportunity I had to give myself away.

"This will only take a few minutes. Let me walk you to the elevator." He swept an arm toward our left. I fell into step beside him, feeling more comfortable. If he knew anything, he gave no indication. "Did you have any questions?"

"No, I don't think so." The previous day had been a whirlwind of procedures, and briefings. Although I'd forgotten quite a few details, the massive stack of non-disclosure agreements wasn't one of them.

"As Mr. Menshikov's personal assistant, you'll need to be aware of our security protocol. I have some self-defense classes set up for you to take this week. Nothing too extensive, just the basics: defensive driving, hostage negotiation, kidnapping prevention."

"You're kidding, right?" Laughter bubbled up my sore throat before I could censor it.

"Not at all. We take personal safety very seriously." Ivan's somber stare killed the smile on my face. "His and yours."

"Yes, of course." What had I gotten myself into? My blood chilled with a different kind of fear, one centered around my well-being. "Is he under some kind of threat? Are we in danger?"

"A man with his kind of history has many enemies, known and unknown. I do my best to diffuse potential threats before they take root, but one can never be too careful."

A cold shiver ran down my back. No wonder Menshikov was so dark. "Whatever I can do to help, please let me know."

"I appreciate that." His expression warmed, making him less threatening and almost handsome. "I did not mean to frighten you. Mr. Menshikov insists that all his employees know how to defend themselves out of his concern for their welfare. We have an excellent security team, one of the best in the world. Let me worry about his safety. You're going to have your hands full with his personal needs. Which leads me to the purpose of this visit. As his closest employee, you'll have access to certain…*aspects*…of his private life that require the utmost discretion."

The way he said *aspects* made my stomach flip. Did Roman have some kind of kinky sex cave in the apartment? I'd heard about billionaires with outlandish sexual proclivities. If the Masquerade de Marquis was any indication, Mr. Menshikov could easily belong to this group. Under that line of reasoning, however, I was just as kinky as he was, something I didn't want to admit.

As if reading my mind, Ivan said, "By now, you've heard of The Devil's Playground?"

My insides began to quake. I nodded, unable to find my voice.

His unnerving stare bored into me. "From time to time, you'll be required to assist in tasks relating to the club. I trust you understand how devastating any leaks of information could be to him or the other members."

"Yes." Thoughts of the naked guests writhing in the great hall turned my musings to Prince Charming, and thoughts of Prince Charming made my thighs clench together. Would I run into him or Nicky during my employment? If Ivan was here, the chances of an encounter grew exponentially. *Stop being a worry wart, Rourke.* No one would recognize me with different hair and the extra weight I'd put on.

"Ms. Donahue?" Ivan asked.

An inferno of embarrassment ignited beneath my skin.

Goodness, I needed to get away from this man and this conversation before I combusted from mortification. "You don't have to worry," I said. "I consider my employer's privacy to be sacred."

By this time, we'd reached the elevator. He pressed the button, and the doors opened immediately. I stepped into the elevator, but he kept the doors from closing with one of his hands. "I trust you'll keep our discussion confidential."

"Of course." We said our goodbyes, and I rode down the elevator to the next floor with my mind awhirl. The Devil's Playground, security teams, self-defense training, and *aspects*? By all accounts, I was in way over my head. This new position threatened to stretch all of my boundaries, both personally and professionally.

I met Julie at my apartment door. She greeted me with a reserved smile. Her burgundy dress and nude sandals exuded comfort without sacrificing style. I tugged on the placket of my blouse. Everly had never had a dress code. Most of the time I'd worn jeans and tennis shoes. I really needed to step up my game if I wanted to fit in around here.

Julie spent the next hour going over the layout of the condo, introducing me to the other staff, and outlining Mr. Menshikov's preferences. Once we'd finished, we rode in a private car over to the Blue Sapphire Building and took another elevator up to the top floor. The doors opened into a sleek reception area.

"This is the executive floor." The shiny locks of her chin-length hair swung with each of her steps. "Your office is this way, next to Mr. Menshikov's."

The heels of our shoes tapped on the black granite floor as we walked. Glass doors slid open at our approach. Aside from our footsteps and the clicking of keyboards, total silence blanketed the office. We passed framed black-and-white photographs and metal sculptures on the way to a wall of frosted glass and more sliding doors.

"These are his office assistants. You'll need to coordinate all of his personal appointments with his work schedule. They'll be instrumental to you. I'll make introductions later." Six identical glass desks flanked the walkway, three on each side. Five women and one man wore headsets, their gazes trained on their computers. The cut of their suits reminded me to ask about the clothing allowance. Next to their smart chic, my worn suit looked dull and frumpy.

We passed the glass wall to a normal black door with silver hardware. Julie turned the knob and motioned me inside. "This is your space. It has a direct entrance into Mr. Menshikov's office. After you go over his schedule each morning at the apartment and between running errands, you'll hang out here and await any further instructions."

Shiny metal and glass surfaces reflected the overhead lights. Blue Sapphire must pay a fortune just to follow employees around and erase fingerprints. I ran a finger over the glass desk, but the view outside the window stole my attention. The morning fog had lifted and provided a rare view of the city. I drew in a sharp, awestruck breath.

"Amazing, isn't it?" Julie asked. She joined me at the window.

"It's unbelievable." The office itself was the size of a large closet, but the view opened up the space.

"You're very lucky to have a view like this. Unfortunately, you won't have much time to enjoy it." She turned, her motions brisk, and logged into the computer with a few taps of the keyboard. "We're still waiting on your computer access from IT. In the meantime, you can run a few errands. I've just emailed the list of tasks to you. It's nothing too difficult. Pick up a few personal items, lunch, and open his mail. You'll find the addresses in the contact list."

My phone dinged with the message. I scanned over the list. "Okay. No problem."

"It's nine o'clock now. You'll need to be back here by noon with his lunch. Don't be late." A line dented her forehead. "He has a conference call with one of his foreign clients at twelve-thirty. Make sure to hold any calls that may come through. He's very particular about interruptions. I've got a doctor's appointment at one. I'll be back afterward to walk through more of your duties then."

"Is everything okay?" I pushed aside my concern to study her face.

"Sure." The paleness of her complexion suggested otherwise. "Just a checkup. No worries." She glanced at her wristwatch and motioned toward the door. "You'd better move if you want to get back on time."

❀

At five minutes after twelve, I rapped on Roman's door adjoining my office. When he didn't answer, I knocked a second time.

"Come in." Irritation laced the command. I squared my shoulders, uncertain of what to expect. His suit jacket had been slung across an arm of the sofa, and he sat in his chair facing the window.

"I've got your lunch, sir," I said.

He swiveled to face me, a study in coiled power and smoldering confidence. The top two buttons of his white dress shirt had been unfastened, revealing a triangle of tanned skin. A bolt of sexual energy hit me between the legs. I blinked at the sudden jolt.

"You're late." Long, elegant fingers drummed on the desk and echoed the beat of my pulse.

I swallowed. Geez this guy was intimidating. "Traffic was

bad today. There's a ton of construction going on."

"Traffic is bad every day," he said. "Plan better next time."

"Yes, sir, I will." I placed the sandwich on the desk in front of him. "Can I get you anything else?"

"Did you pick up my tuxedo?" The paper crinkled as he unwrapped the sandwich. I nodded, my throat raw. "Hang it on the back of my bedroom door." A scowl darkened his face and sent a tremor down my legs. "What the fuck is this?" He pulled the bread apart and showed the surface to me.

"Um, mustard?"

"Yellow mustard. I don't eat yellow mustard. I specifically asked for Dijon. What part of that is so difficult?"

"Nothing. That's what I ordered." With shaking hands, I dug in my pocket for my phone and called up the order. "See? Dijon."

The line of his shoulders fell. He tossed the sandwich in the trash.

I tried to keep my expression neutral. "Would you like me to get you something else?"

"It's too late. Just go back to your office." He flicked his hand toward my door. "Wait."

I stopped in my tracks and curbed a sigh of exasperation. This man was a true piece of work. Everly would die when I told her. She'd been easy to work with, probably because we'd known each other for so long. I'd been able to anticipate her needs without asking, but this man—he baffled me at every turn. Before answering, I smoothed my expression. "Yes?"

"This call from Germany. It's very important, and I don't want any interruptions. Hold my calls. No exceptions. Do you think you can do that, Rita?"

"Absolutely." My patience began to fray around the edges. "And my name is Rourke."

He didn't answer, and I didn't turn around. Instead, I

stormed to my office and flopped behind the desk. I'd heard about the diva behavior of other employers from peers but had never expected to find myself in this kind of situation. The urge to quit stormed through my head. Screw him and his Dijon mustard. Then my personal phone hummed with a voice mail. I checked it.

"Hi, Rourke. This is Nurse Johnson from the Parkview Retirement Home. Do you think you could stop by this evening? Your aunt is having a particularly hard time today. Seeing you might do her some good."

There it was—my reason for suffering through the unbearable behavior of Mr. Roman Jackass Menshikov. Aunt Grace suffered from early onset Alzheimer's. After the police had found her wandering the streets in her bathrobe, I'd been forced to find full-time care, and it didn't come cheaply.

The office phone at my elbow lit up with several incoming calls. I shoved aside my misgivings. Until something better came along, I intended to give one hundred percent to this job.

"Mr. Menshikov's office. This is Rourke speaking." I put on a smile and used my most upbeat tone.

"Hi, this is Milada. Can I speak to Mr. Menshikov?" a high-pitched female voice requested. She sounded young, too young to be calling an adult man.

I wrinkled my nose. Is this what Ivan had meant by *aspects*? My blood chilled at the thought. "I'm sorry. He's in a meeting. Can I take a message?"

"No. I mean, well, yes. Just tell him Milada called, his daughter."

I sat up in my chair. The hot ogre had a daughter? "Wait. If you really need him, I'll go interrupt his meeting."

"Um, yes, please."

I placed the call on hold, knocked on his door, then entered. He was pacing in front of the window. Thumb and forefinger pinched the bridge of his nose. When I opened the door, he scowled and covered the mouthpiece of his Bluetooth with a hand. I cleared my throat. "I'm sorry to interrupt."

"Then get out," he said. Blue eyes shot ice daggers in my direction.

"But I think you want—"

"Out!" His shout vibrated down to my toes. "Don't make me tell you again."

I scurried into the other room. No one had ever shouted at me like that before, and never in my place of employment. It took everything I had to keep from storming out the door. When he got off his call, we needed to have a serious talk. After a deep exhale, I picked up the phone call, but Milada was gone.

An hour later, Julie returned from her doctor's appointment. Mr. Menshikov stormed into my office, nostrils flaring and the color high on his cheekbones.

I sucked up my courage. "I'm sorry for interrupting your call, but your daughter called," I said, and watched the color drain from his face.

"Milada?" The name fell reverently from his lips.

"Yes. I—"

"Is she on the phone now?"

I shook my head. "I came back to take a message, but she was gone."

"Damn it!" A tide of red swept up his neck. I'd never seen a man so angry before, or so incredibly hot. His nostrils flared, and a vein stood out in his forehead. Every line of his lean body vibrated with masculine irritation. With visible effort, he straightened his shoulders and pointed a finger at Julie. "You. In my office. Now."

The door slammed behind them. Even with a wall between us, I could hear every word, and so could the rest of the staff. I winced at each shout. Mortification burned through my body, followed by the sting of ice-cold rejection. He was going to fire me. Maybe it was for the best. Then I remembered my aunt, my lack of residence, and the dwindling dollars in my bank account.

"I want her gone," he said. "Today. Before she fucks up anything else."

I couldn't hear Julie's part of the conversation, but it was easy enough to fill in the blanks. An eternity later, she came into my office and placed a hand on my shoulder. "It's okay. You had no way of knowing. He's been on edge for a while now. His ex has been hiding their daughter from him. He hasn't talked to her in weeks, and he's been worried sick. This is the first time he's heard from her."

"I tried to tell him," I said, weakly, fighting against the churn of acid in my stomach.

"He'll cool down. Please don't let this deter you from staying." Behind her plea, green colored her complexion, and her smile had lost some of its sparkle.

"Are you okay, Julie? Maybe you should sit down."

"I appreciate your concern. I'll be fine." The waver in her voice suggested otherwise, but I didn't pry. She'd tell me if she wished. "Why don't you take the rest of the afternoon off and go shopping with your clothing allowance?"

"Sure. I'll do that." Several different emotions warred against each other. Part of me understood Menshikov's distress, but another part of me burned with indignation. No one had ever talked to me like that before, and I didn't like it.

Julie left with the promise to continue my training tomorrow. I finished adding a few new appointments to Mr. Menshikov's calendar. With each passing minute, my anger escalated. How dare he talk to me that way? I was neither incompetent nor stupid. I gathered my purse and knocked on his door.

"What?" he asked, his voice low and rough.

It wasn't an invitation, but I entered anyway. The sight of him stopped me in my tracks. He was seated behind his desk, elbows on his knees, head resting in his hands, the picture of dejection. The inferno in my belly lowered to a flickering flame, but I held my ground. "I need to speak with you."

A huge sigh lifted his shoulders. He sat up but didn't look at me. I walked around his desk until the tips of my toes faced his. For the first time, our eyes met. A jolt of electricity traveled down my body and into my womb. The shock was quickly replaced by sympathy. The depths of his eyes were no longer icy, but liquid and dark and filled with remorse. He was hurting inside.

"Go on." Resignation and defeat laced his tone. He shifted back in the chair. Faint shadows smudged beneath his eyes, shadows I'd failed to notice before.

"I understand you're upset about the call. I feel terrible about it, but in my defense, I tried to tell you, and you threw me out." A violent trembling shook my hands. I pressed my palms together, determined to have my say. "You need to know that I take my job very seriously. If you give me instructions, I'll do my best to follow them. In return, I need to be treated with respect." He drew in a breath, like he was about to speak, but I blundered on. "I'm more than capable of doing this job. Everly trusted me to run her personal life for six years, and I did a damn good job of it. I can assure you I'll never give you any less than one hundred percent effort, but you have to give me important information. I'm not psychic." Thinking I might have crossed a line with my last comment, I bit my lower lip.

"Everly?" A flicker of interest crossed his face. "That's right. You worked for Everly Martin."

"Yes. We…"

A new kind of interest flared in his scrutiny. For the first time, he looked at me, *really* looked, from the tips of my shoes to the top of my head. I felt his gaze, solid as a touch. When those dark eyes scoured my face, I had to glance away, certain my forehead displayed every thought in my head like a scrolling marquee.

"It's okay." With a wave of his hand, he gestured for me to stop talking. "I should have been more explicit in my instructions. I'll have Julie give you a more detailed list of my personal contacts in order of priority."

"Thank you. It's appreciated." The lack of animosity in his tone put me on alert. I'd expected more yelling and insults. This twist of personality confused me more than ever. Maybe he was schizophrenic.

"In the future, if Milada calls, I want you to interrupt me. My daughter takes precedence over everyone and everything else. Understand?"

"Yes." Apparently, Satan had a heart after all. Curiosity nibbled at my composure. I had to bite back a dozen questions. Did he have an ex-wife? Why did they split up?

"I'll be out of the office for the next couple of days. Something unexpected has come up." With his hand on the small of my back, he ushered me toward the door. The light touch reminded me of Prince Charming and the way he'd escorted me around the masquerade with his hand in that very spot. An excited shiver snaked up my spine. "You can use this time to get up to speed, and we'll talk when I return."

"Okay. I'll do that." A mixture of hopefulness, excitement, and wariness bubbled in my veins.

"And see a doctor about that cold. I need you healthy." His hand lingered on my back.

I blinked up at him, turned on by his touch, confused by his concern, and irritated by the rapid vacillation of his emotions.

"Hey, hey." A man met us at the door, his hand poised in the air, ready to knock.

"Nikolay. You should have called," Menshikov said.

The air seemed to vacate the room. I stared up into the wide gray eyes of Nicky, looking more delicious than I remembered. A dark pair of jeans hung low on his narrow hips. He pushed up the sleeves of his burgundy sweater and ran a hand through his windswept hair while sliding a glance up and down my figure. "Well, hello. You're new."

"This is Rona, my assistant," Menshikov said.

"Rourke." His continued refusal to remember my name ignited my temper again. The muscles in my forehead tensed. If I hadn't been in shock over Nicky's appearance, I would have erupted. "It's Rourke Donahue. Nice to meet you." Surely Nicky wouldn't see past my glasses and shorter, darker hair.

"The pleasure is all mine." Taking my hand in his, he brushed a kiss over my knuckles. "You'll have to forgive Roman for not introducing us. My name is Nikolay Reznik, but my friends call me Nicky. *You* may call me Nicky, too." A pleasant warmth crept up my arm until his thumb brushed over the amethyst ring on my little finger. The moisture left my mouth. His eyes lifted to mine. Recognition sparked in their depths. I withdrew my hand and dropped it into my pocket. Mischief curled the corners of his lips.

"Ms. Donahue was just leaving." By his tone, Mr. Menshikov frowned upon fraternization between his friends and employees. I'd have to check the employment contract. At least he remembered my last name this time.

"Have we met before, Ms. Donahue?" Nicky asked.

"No." To hide my anxiety, I dropped my gaze to the floor, trapped between two mouthwatering men, unable to escape.

"Are you sure? I never forget a face."

"I'm sure. I'd remember if we had." I mustered a polite

smile and pushed past the men. "It was nice to meet you."

❧

*O*n the ride to my aunt's nursing home, I stared into space. The last person I'd expected to see today was Nicky. I twirled the amethyst ring around my finger, over and over and over. There had been no mistaking the recognition in his smirk. In the background, the rhythmic clicking of the subway melded with the screech of metal and the hum of conversation and mimicked the chaos in my head. Would he tell Roman that I'd crashed his party? I ran through a thousand different scenarios of how that scene might play out. All of them ended with Roman screwing me on his sparkling glass desk and a blush on my cheeks.

When I arrived at the nursing home, the sight of my aunt sitting on her suitcase by the curb straightened out my priorities. A summer breeze fluttered the hem of her floral print cotton dress. She smiled as I approached.

"Auntie? What are you doing?" A box of personal items sat at her feet. The sight of her, small and a shadow of her former self, squeezed my heart.

"I'm going home."

"This is home. You live here now, remember?" Confusion passed over her face, like a cloud drifting in front of the sun. "Come on. I'll get your bag."

"No. I want to go home." I didn't recognize the sharpness in her voice. My aunt had always been kind and soft spoken and teeming with warmth. This crazy disease twisted everything.

"You can't go back. You sold the house last year, remember?" How long had she been sitting outside in the hot sun? I glanced around for a nurse or security guard but saw no one.

"No." Auntie passed a trembling hand across her forehead, and my heart ached for her. "What about Tim? Does he know?"

"Let's get inside and we can talk about it, okay?" With a gentle touch, I looped her arm through mine and guided her back to her room. She sat on the edge of the bed and stared at her hands like they belonged to someone else. Pain sliced across my chest, razor-sharp and crystal-clear.

"I need to see Tim. Will you call him for me?"

Unshed tears burned my sore throat. I dredged up a smile, took her hand in mine, and patted it. "Uncle Tim passed away, Auntie, four years ago. You know that, right?"

We'd been over it a hundred times before, but every time was like the first time for her. She sobbed on my shoulder. Her tears left a dark, wet circle on my shirt. Alzheimer's was like a surging wave, sweeping in and eroding the coastline of her memories. Chunks of her past disappeared each day. It killed me to see the once-shrewd woman reduced to an uncertain child.

When her tears ceased, I tucked her into bed and went to see the nurse in charge. "What's going on?" I asked. "How did she get outside like that? She could have wandered away. Why wasn't anyone watching her?"

"We're understaffed," the nurse said. "Most of us are working double shifts. There just aren't enough of us to go around. And your aunt, she can be difficult."

I sympathized with her problem, but it didn't make me feel any better. "This is unacceptable. I pay you to watch over her. If you can't keep her safe, then I'm going to have to move her somewhere else."

The nurse shrugged at my hollow threat. We both knew there weren't any other places available, at least none my aunt could afford. Even with my new job and raise, it would take months to get her into a new facility. I'd just have to pray that fate would provide an answer for us.

CHAPTER 13

ROURKE

*W*hen Menshikov returned three days later, I accompanied Jose, the driver, to the airport with a hot coffee and a copy of *The Wall Street Journal*. We drove straight onto the tarmac and parked next to a sleek blue-and-silver private jet. Butterflies tumbled in my stomach. In Roman's absence, I'd been given a crash course on his personal preferences, lifestyle, and basic needs. No amount of studying, however, could prepare me for his temper. I drew in a deep breath and pressed my palms together.

"Here he comes," said Jose in his thick, nasally Brooklyn accent. "Ivan says he's in a pissy mood today. Better buckle your seat belt. It's going to be a bumpy ride home."

"Great," I muttered and steeled my nerves.

Sunshine reflected off the clean surface of the jet. I squinted against the brightness, adjusting my sunglasses, and stared at the open door of the plane. A dark head appeared through the opening. My employer stepped out, wearing a baseball cap, sunglasses, white polo shirt and jeans. Heat shimmered over the pavement. Something twisted in my gut. I made a strangled noise and grabbed the door handle.

"You okay?" Jose glanced at me in the rearview mirror. His bushy eyebrows and warm brown eyes reminded me of my dad.

"Um, yes. I'm fine." But nothing could have been further from the truth. The man striding across the tarmac had a confident, graceful stride. Black aviators hid his eyes, and four days' growth of beard softened the strong line of his chin. He slung his jacket over his shoulder and closed the distance between us. I might have been able to convince myself otherwise before, but not now. Menshikov was undeniably, unmistakably, one hundred percent my Prince Charming. "Oh, shit," I mumbled, not caring if the driver heard me.

If he noticed, he didn't have time to remark. He jumped out of the car, crossed to the opposite side, and opened the door. "Good afternoon, Mr. Menshikov. It's good to have you back, sir."

Hot summer air rushed through the open door. I stared, mouth dry, and tried not to panic. *Breathe, Rourke. Breathe.* Warm, soothing air rushed through my nose and out my mouth. Everly had used the technique to calm her stage fright before a speech. I wasn't sure why. All it did was make me dizzy.

"Is that my coffee?" he asked as he slid across the gray leather seat.

Unable to speak, my voice robbed by shock, I thrust the Styrofoam cup into his outstretched hand. The cabin filled with his clean, intoxicating scent, the same cologne worn by Prince Charming. How had I not noticed? Maybe because my nose had been clogged by a cold and my head muddled by a six-figure salary. He sat across from me, knees spread wide, one arm slung across the back of the seat. A curious vibration hummed through my body, buzzing like bees in my blood. I removed my sunglasses and pretended to clean a speck from the mirrored lenses.

"I've got some serious jet lag," he said in his rich voice, a voice that had murmured hot, dirty things into my ear. After two gulps from the cup, he set the coffee in the drink holder and trained his gaze on me. Even though I couldn't see his eyes, I knew he was watching me. The weight of his stare slid over my new wrap dress and down my bare legs. I pressed my thighs together to curb the sudden ache between them.

"How was London?" I asked to break the awkward tension, and put my sunglasses back on my nose.

"Rained the whole time." With a subtle shift of his weight, he turned to observe the blue sky and sunshine outside the window. He extended his phone to me. "Charge this up, would you? I'm down to ten percent."

"Sure." I dug through my bag for the charger with trembling hands. When I finally found it, it took several tries before I could plug the end into the limo's USB port. His relentless stare didn't help matters.

"I'm going to Edinburgh next month. I need you to make sure everything is arranged. Can you do that?" The smooth timbre of his voice washed over me.

I swallowed and nodded while tapping a reminder into my phone. Julie had given me a list of his favorite hotels and restaurants. He shifted again and rested both hands lightly on the tops of his thighs. From behind the shield of my sunglasses, I stared at the neat, square tips of his fingers, fingers that had been inside me. The moisture left my mouth. I dragged my tongue over the dry surface of my lips.

"Is this for business or pleasure?" I asked.

He snorted. "It's always both. Why do you ask?"

"I'll need to make sure you have the right clothes." I kept my head down to avoid staring at his handsome face. "Will you be traveling alone?"

"No." His fingers drummed a restless beat on his immaculate pants. "You're coming with me."

CHAPTER 14

ROMAN

*J*ose opened the car door and nodded in greeting. The first thing I saw was a long stretch of feminine calf, nude peep-toe pumps, and delicate pink polished toes visible through the opening. I followed the line of her legs up to a narrow waist and high, perfect breasts. Silver sunglasses hid her eyes, but there was no mistaking that mouth. I'd dreamed a hundred times of fisting my hand in her hair and ravishing those pouty lips. *Cinderella's lips.*

No wonder Nicky had been having fits. She'd been in front of me this whole time. I'd been a fool not to see it before. The stupidity stung my pride, and it served me right. I'd been too arrogant, too selfish, too absorbed in my problems to look at her, *really* look at her. For most of my life, I'd run over the people beneath me, using them as tools to further my personal agenda, discarding them when their usefulness abated. At first glance, she'd been a nuisance, another dim-witted assistant, someone to serve my needs. I shoved a hand in my hair and hesitated before sliding onto the seat.

The blue of her dress highlighted eyes the color of a hot summer sky, and those lips... I shifted in the seat to ease the pressure behind the fly of my pants. Her hair was darker and shorter, and she'd gained a few pounds in all the right places, but there was no mistaking that mouth. And I'd been a total and complete ass to her from the start.

Inches separated my knee from hers. The heat of her body radiated up my leg, escalating my torture. We stumbled through some inane conversation while I tried to get a grip on the current situation. I found Ivan's number in my contacts and dialed. He answered on the first ring.

"You must think you're pretty smart," I said, my eyes glued to Rourke's face.

"Ah, so you finally figured it out." Amusement brightened the cadence of his speech. "I wondered how many days it would take before you dragged your nose away from your computer long enough to see that your mystery woman has been in front of you all this time."

"I'm glad I was able to entertain you."

Rourke shifted in the seat. The hem of her dress hiked up her thigh. I closed my eyes and swallowed, remembering how it had felt to be between those legs, how willing and wet her pussy had been for me.

"It's been a delight," Ivan said. "And to think you tried to fire her on the first day. Classic Roman. I hope you've learned your lesson."

"What lesson is that? Not to trust you anymore?"

Rourke tugged her skirt down toward her knees. Her skin glowed with good health and a hint of summer sun. Desire twitched my fingers. What I wouldn't give to run a hand up the inside of her leg, up her thigh, to caress that smooth flesh.

"You must have gotten a good laugh," I continued.

His heavy sigh gusted against the phone. "Grow up, Roman. It's time."

The phone call ended in a dial tone. He always had to have the last word, in every damn situation. I placed the phone back on the seat to finish charging and stared at Rourke. She'd replaced her sunglasses, cutting off access to her expressive eyes, and stared out the window. Now that I knew who she was, I couldn't get enough of her. I drank in every inch of her body, her legs, her face. My princess was sitting in the limousine across from me, and there wasn't a freaking thing I could do about it without courting a sexual harassment suit.

"What did you do while I was gone?" I asked.

"Um, well, I spent some time with Ivan learning self-defense, and Julie got me up to speed on your email accounts. We set up a tentative list of tasks, subject to your approval, and—"

I cut her off with an uplifted palm. "No. I mean, what did you do outside of work?"

She brushed her hair behind her ears and pursed her lips. "I had lunch with a few friends and went shopping for clothes."

I burned with jealousy at the thought of her laughing and cutting up with people who knew her better than I did. What would it take to win her over, to become one of her trusted circle? After showing my ass to her, the probability seemed slight. Even if I managed to overcome the hurdle of my bad behavior, I'd have to fire her before I could fuck her, because I never screwed my employees.

I stared at her, contemplating a new and disturbing thought. Did she know I was the man at the masquerade? If she knew, she'd done one hell of a job covering it up. I studied her closed posture—arms barricaded over her chest, legs crossed and pointed away from me, the serious line of her mouth. The more I stared at her, the more I wanted her. She represented the ultimate challenge, a woman who didn't want me. However, I always got what I wanted. Always. And Rourke Donahue had just become my next conquest.

CHAPTER 15

ROURKE

For the next seven hours, I tried to anticipate Roman's needs while avoiding conversation, and he made a noticeable effort not to insult me. During his time in London, something had shifted in his demeanor. Sometimes I caught him watching me, pensive and brooding, brows lowered. Other times, he stared openly, and I had the distinct feeling he could see straight through my clothing. Most of the time, he ignored me, which I took as a blessing. The less interaction between us, the less chance of him recognizing our previous acquaintance.

At the end of the day, we went straight from the office to an elegant country club for a dinner meeting. I welcomed the buffer of other people to ease the tension between us. His brooding blue eyes threatened to get the best of my composure. And I couldn't afford to let him get to me.

When the waiter attempted to pull out a chair for me, Roman motioned him aside and slid the seat beneath my legs. The unexpected thoughtfulness of the gesture took me by surprise. Until today, he'd barely acknowledged my existence. I gave him a tight smile, avoiding eye contact, and tried to calm the butterflies in my belly.

Roman's guests arrived on our heels. The scent of old money clung to their conservative clothes and cool stares. I forced a pleasant smile but felt it slip when the woman turned to face me. Her delicate features, black hair, and large bosom were shockingly familiar. This was the woman from The Devil's Playground, the one with the elaborate plumed mask.

"Ms. Donahue, I'd like you to meet the Weavers—Henry and Deborah," Roman said.

The man smiled and shook my hand. The overhead chandeliers glinted off his bald head. Deborah's gaze flicked over Roman's hand on the back of my chair. He cleared his throat and dropped his hand, curling his fingers into a fist.

"It's a pleasure to meet you," I said, but they'd already turned their attention to Roman. Despite my years as a personal assistant, I'd never gotten used to the glass wall separating me from the upper class. Everly had always treated me like a friend and family member. But her business colleagues and acquaintances had not. Most of them ignored me. None of them made eye contact. Their censure irritated more than it wounded. I didn't need their approval to bolster my self-confidence, but a little common courtesy would have been nice.

"Darling, you're looking wonderful." Deborah tried to air-kiss Roman's cheeks, but he stepped away, leaving her lips pursed in midair. I stifled a laugh.

After everyone was seated, the waiter opened a bottle of wine for Roman's approval. The conversation drifted from current events to sports and, finally, to vacation hot spots. I couldn't concentrate with Roman's knee brushing mine beneath the table every few minutes. My senses went into a state of hyperawareness. Every shift of his body, every rise and fall of his chest, sent arousal flooding through my veins. Why did he have to be so handsome? Despite an overseas flight and back-to-back conference calls, his gaze remained predatory and sharp. I marveled at his ability to focus when I could only think about ruinous castles, masked strangers, and sex, sex, sex.

"We spent the summer in Ibiza last year," Deborah said, in a pronounced Bostonian accent. "The beaches were amazing. The people were beautiful. You should go there, Roman." The patronizing smirk on her red lips raised my hackles. She patted my hand. "If you're lucky, maybe he'll take you with him, sweetheart."

Throughout the meal, no one had addressed me directly. Her touch brought me back from the depths of Roman's blue eyes. I swallowed, aware that I'd been ogling him, and scrambled to gather my thoughts.

"Have you been to Ibiza, Rourke?" Roman dabbed a napkin to his full lower lip. My gaze locked on his mouth. Memories of his kisses consumed me, the taste of his tongue, the softness of his mouth. "What do you think? Is it worth my trouble?"

"Ibiza is lovely but a little too crowded for my taste." I took a sip of wine to clear the erotic images from my head before speaking again. "You might like Anse Source d'Argent in Seychelles better. It's quiet and peaceful. I'd love to go back again sometime."

The woman's eyes narrowed, her tone disbelieving. "I've never heard of it. I suppose we'll have to check it out, won't we, Henry?" Her gaze turned to her husband.

A sip of wine went down the wrong pipe, and I sputtered.

Roman thumped my back. "Are you alright?"

"Yes." I cleared my throat and tried to look anywhere but at the couple across the table. Visions of the woman in the grand hall, her arms and feet in restraints, bent over the velvet bench, burned the backs of my eyes. The man pounding into her had not been her husband. Did he know? Did he care? Adultery under any circumstances made my stomach queasy.

"I haven't had a vacation in a very long time," Roman said. His hand returned to the back of my chair. The tips of his fingers brushed my shoulder. A frisson of electricity jolted up my neck. I shivered. He withdrew his hand to his lap. The muscles of his jaw flexed.

"Maybe Ms. Donahue will be kind enough to arrange a visit for all of us." The woman's sharp gaze noticed my reaction to his touch. Her mouth turned down. "Henry and I enjoy your company. We haven't spent nearly enough time together this year."

The proprietary bite of her tone was unmistakable. A new and disturbing notion soured the taste of dinner. I dropped my fork to the table and nodded to the waiter. He removed the plate with white-gloved hands. Had Roman been involved with this woman? Something in their easy demeanor confirmed my suspicions.

"Have you vacationed together before?" I asked, directing the question to my employer.

"Roman has been kind enough to invite us to his home in London for the past few years." She stared at me. Did she recognize me? I ignored the unpleasant notion and kept my gaze trained on Roman.

"Like I said, I haven't had a vacation in a very long time." The line of tension between us tightened until I couldn't breathe. "But I enjoy opening my estates to business associates and friends. Just because I don't have time to enjoy them doesn't mean they should go unoccupied."

"You're generous beyond words," Henry said, joining the conversation once more. If he'd been bothered by his wife's statements, he didn't show it in expression or tone. Maybe he approved of her indiscretions. Maybe he liked to watch. Heat raced up my neck, raising my temperature to the point of discomfort.

"Have you been to the London manor yet? It's quite exceptional."

"Um, no. I've never been there." The lie soured on my tongue.

"Really? Are you sure? I could have sworn I saw you there in the spring." The weight of her stare burned through me. I stared back, unblinking, refusing to be intimidated.

"This is only my second week with Mr. Menshikov." I twisted in my chair, desperate to escape this line of questioning. She knew.

"Enough idle conversation." Roman gestured for the waiters to clear the first course from the table. "Let's talk business." Without looking in my direction, he dropped his napkin on the table. "Rourke, I don't think I'll need you tonight after all. Have Jose take you home. I'll catch a cab later."

The abrupt dismissal stung. I blinked but nodded. A smug smile flitted across the woman's face. With stiff movements, I pushed my chair from the table and stood. "Thank you for dinner. Good evening."

I walked to the door, feeling humiliated and raw. Maybe this job had been a huge mistake. The walls of my throat constricted. I swallowed back tears. Why was I so emotional? I wasn't Roman's date. I was his personal assistant. If I wanted to succeed in this position, I needed to remember my place. Knowing his identity changed everything.

CHAPTER 16

ROMAN

I had to send Rourke away. For the past hour, I'd been in a constant state of arousal. Our thighs kept bumping into each other beneath the table. Every brush of her knee against mine sent blood rushing into my cock. My balls ached and my temper simmered. The knowledge of how it felt to be inside her proved to be a major distraction. I needed to be on my game during this meeting, something I couldn't do with her sitting beside me.

"She's nice—plain—but sweet," Deborah said, her dark gaze roving over me as Rourke exited the dining room.

"Yes, lovely girl," said her husband.

Like always, his words echoed his wife's sentiments. The poor man didn't have one thought to claim as his own. Deborah was the brains behind their enterprise. Her wit and intelligence had attracted me when we first met. Back then, I'd had little respect for the sanctity of marriage. Milada's mother had seen to that. Time and maturity had changed my feelings on the topic, however.

Deborah's eyes narrowed. "How long will she last, I wonder? She doesn't seem to have the backbone necessary to put up with someone like you." Despite the teasing quality of her tone, the words stung. They sliced into my soft underbelly, catching me by surprise. She placed a hand on my forearm. "Should we place a bet?"

"I'm in for a thousand." Her husband's eyes brightened. "I give her a week."

"This one is different, though." Deborah studied my face. I stared back at her, wondering why I'd ever found her poisonous personality attractive. "I give her a month. And let's make it two thousand, shall we?"

I shook off her hand and dropped it into her lap. "You're skating on thin ice. Both of you." Although Rourke and I had gotten off to a rocky start, the need to protect her from needless ridicule consumed me. The color drained from beneath Deborah's fake tan. "If you're trying to coax additional funding out of me for your project, this isn't the way to go about it. To avoid any future misunderstandings, my employees are not for your amusement."

"Since when do you give a crap about your employees?" Her observation made me straighten in my chair. She and her husband both shifted away from me. "The old Roman used to love a good wager."

"My behavior back then was irresponsible and callous." Beneath my bravado, I knew she was right. The number of personal assistants left in my wake proved it. "I've learned from my mistakes. You should do the same. Now, are you done wasting my time?"

She rolled her lips together and dropped her gaze to the table. Fear flickered in her eyes. "I apologize. We were only trying to have a little fun."

"Not at my expense or Ms. Donahue's." I let my words sink in for a few seconds before shifting the topic to business. Maybe I'd been an ass to my former assistants, but I could do better. Finding my Cinderella had changed every-thing. I had to improve or risk losing her forever.

❀

*I*n the limo the next morning, on our way to the office, Rourke sat across from me, the picture of self-restraint and cool composure. I pretended to scroll through emails, but watched her through the veil of my eyelashes. She uncrossed and crossed her legs, sending a shockwave of need into my groin. To make matters worse, her amazing scent, clean and citrusy, filled the car. I shifted to ease the stiffness behind the fly of my trousers. With her hair in a bun at the nape of her neck and her blouse buttoned to her chin, she looked like an uptight schoolteacher—a sexy, needs-a-good-fuck schoolteacher. In another life, I would have pulled the pins from her hair, popped the buttons of her blouse and tested her limits in every dirty way possible. Instead, I settled back in my seat and blew out a frustrated sigh.

"What?" A pink tide crept up her neck. She tucked a strand of hair behind her ear. It was inappropriate to stare, but I couldn't stop wondering if she had a boyfriend, if she dated, if she'd ever been married. I wanted to ask but it was none of my business.

"Your outfit—I approve. Very professional." The color intensified to a dusty rose and settled in her cheeks.

On her first day of work, my assessment of her wardrobe had been harsh but absolutely necessary. In my line of work, appearances meant everything. The minute I stepped into a boardroom, judgements were made and opinions formed. If I showed up for a multi-million-dollar acquisition dressed in worn shoes and shabby jeans, my partners would question my competence. This business existed in a game of smoke and mirrors, and I'd become an expert player.

The limo rounded a corner. Rourke extended a hand to keep her balance. The shift in movement caused her straight black skirt to hike above her knees. She tugged on the hem and crossed her legs again, drawing my focus to her smooth skin and the freckle above her knee.

"Thanks. One of my friends is a stylist. He put together a wardrobe for me."

He? A prickle of jealousy lifted the hairs on the back of my neck. Who was this guy? How long had they been friends? Dozens of questions lingered on the tip of my tongue. Before I could devise an appropriate way to inquire, her phone rang. She picked up the call. My ears perked at the sound of her smooth, soothing voice. I liked listening to her talk.

"No. That won't work. Mr. Menshikov requires a view of Lake Michigan." Her breasts rose and fell with each breath, perfect and perky beneath the ruffles of her white silk blouse. My fingers flexed involuntarily. Slanting eyebrows drew together over the bridge of her nose. "Is that a suite?" After a pause, her tone grew steely. "No problem. If you can't accommodate us, I'm sure the Four Seasons will have something available."

I put down the phone and stared openly. Her pink lips bowed and a dimple appeared beside her mouth. A bolt of lust hit me squarely below the belt. That mouth, those dimples. The muscles in my throat tightened.

"Yes? Great. The Presidential Suite will be perfect. Could you send over a menu? Mr. Menshikov will be dining in. Thank you." She ended the call with a satisfied smirk. "I got you into the Waldorf. No small feat, considering you only gave me a day's notice."

Getting the Presidential Suite at the Waldorf at the last minute was next to impossible. Although she'd only been with me a short time, she'd already proved her competence by achieving tasks like this one. "I never expected anything less," I said, not to belittle her accomplishment, but to test her. A spark of temper illuminated her eyes; something I'd begun to crave. Occasionally, I called her into my office and picked a fight just so I could see those blue eyes flash. In my world, most people bent over backwards to accommodate my wishes and molded their opinions to echo mine. Not Rourke. Seeing myself through her eyes made want to be a different man—a better man.

"They're faxing over the menu. If you'll pick out what you like, I'll have your meals prepped." She dropped her gaze to the phone on her lap. I felt the loss of those pretty blue irises immediately.

"You decide." I turned my attention back to the phone.

"Are you sure? I might do something stupid like order yellow mustard for your sandwich instead of Grey Poupon."

I glanced up, faking a glower, loving her sass and fearless rebuke. "Are you mocking me, Ms. Donahue?"

"Just stating a fact, Mr. Menshikov."

We shared a smile, our first, and it was the best damn gift I'd received in years.

CHAPTER 17

ROURKE

hen a week had passed without any major incidents, I began to relax and let my guard down. If Roman knew my identity, he didn't let on. In fact, he barely acknowledged my presence, except to bark orders. My pride still smarted from his abrupt dismissal after dinner with the Weavers, but I tried to push aside the affront. After all, he was my employer, not my boyfriend. If I was going to last in this job, I had to get over my crush.

One day after work, as we rode the elevator to the penthouse, I closed my eyes and daydreamed. It was all too easy to forget reality with Roman standing beside me. What if he was my boyfriend? What if we were coming home after a date instead of a long day at the office? The scent of his cologne and aftershave filled my nose. I drew in a deep breath, savoring his manly scent. He shifted his briefcase from one hand to the other, and his shoulder brushed my arm. My eyes flew open to find him watching my reflection in the polished steel door.

"Tired?" he asked, almost like he cared, and God, I wished

he did. I wanted those enigmatic blue eyes to burn with lust and concern for no one but me.

"A little," I said, and moved to the far wall, away from the temptation of his tall, lean body. "It was a long day."

"Yes." He glanced at his watch then at the digital numbers above the door.

I swallowed against the dryness in my throat. Every minute alone with him tested the strength of my self-control. My fingers tightened around the handle of my briefcase. We finished the ascent in silence. The doors slid open. Roman stepped to one side, allowing me to exit first. My high heels clicked on the marble floor while my backside burned under his scrutiny. The butler opened the penthouse doors.

"Good evening, Mr. Menshikov, Ms. Donahue." He extended a hand for Roman's briefcase.

"Good evening." Roman shrugged out of his jacket and tossed it on a chair. A maid scurried to retrieve it before melting into the shadows. He tugged on the knot of his tie then unbuttoned the top two buttons of his shirt. That simple act and the sight of the exposed notch of his collarbone made my sex pulse with desire. I tripped over the edge of the rug. Roman caught my elbow. "Easy there."

"Thanks." Heat scalded my face. I cleared my throat. "Well, if you'll excuse me, I have a few personal matters to take care of." I wanted to call Aunt May. Even though our phone conversations often lacked substance, the sound of her voice offered comfort, and I hoped my voice did the same for her.

"Hang on a second." His deep command hit all the right places inside me. Our eyes met while his agile fingers dropped his diamond and platinum cufflinks into a bowl near the sofa. Watching him roll up his shirtsleeves nearly buckled my knees. Even his forearms were sexy with their slight dusting of black hair and strong, lean muscles. When he'd finished tempting me, he went straight to the liquor cabinet and poured two fingers of vodka from a crystal decanter. "Would you like something, Ms. Donahue?"

"Um, no, thank you." After spending the day in close proximity with him, a drink sounded heavenly, but I couldn't trust myself. Liquor tended to loosen my tongue, as well as my inhibitions.

"Suit yourself." He tossed down the drink, refilled the glass, then sank into the nearest leather armchair with a groan. The ice tinkled against the glass as he swirled the vodka around and around. Finally, he lifted his gaze to mine. "Do you know anything about young girls, Ms. Donahue?"

"No. Not really." I shifted from one foot to the other. The balls of my feet burned from twelve consecutive hours of work. "I'm an only child, and I don't have any friends with children."

"My daughter's birthday is today. I'd like to get her something special, even though—" He stopped midsentence and began again, his smooth voice faltering. "I'd like to get her something nice. Can you help me?"

"It must be hard to be away from her." A sudden pang of sympathy squeezed my heart. For all of his arrogance and confidence, the desperation in his words struck a chord inside me. I wanted to touch his cheek, to offer words of comfort, to do something to lessen his pain. Instead, I froze and stared at the painting over his left shoulder.

"I feel like my fucking heart has been ripped out." He ran a hand through his hair, ruffling the black locks, and sighed. "And I can't do a goddam thing about it."

"I'd love to help. What did you have in mind?" From the edge of the chair across from him, I waited for his answer. Meanwhile, the lump in my throat grew larger and more uncomfortable.

"She's a bit of a tomboy." The sober line of his mouth softened, the corners turning up in amusement. "She likes horses and soccer and her favorite color is green." An incredible softness overtook his sharp features. I blew out a breath, stunned by the transformation. Angry, smoldering Roman Menshikov held a potent kind of charm, but this tender and introspective man made my heart gallop and my panties dampen. "At least, she did. I haven't seen her in a while. Kids change so quickly."

"I'll see what I can do." I gave him a reassuring smile and stood on wobbly legs.

"Thank you." His gaze turned to the wall of windows and the twinkling city lights outside. A chill settled in the room. I shivered and got to my feet. "That will be all, Ms. Donahue."

"Good night." I left him there, in his chair, alone in the darkness, when every cell in my body screamed to pull him into my arms. This man tied my insides into a knot. With every passing day, I tumbled deeper and deeper into a vortex of desire and desperation. And I knew, with all my heart, that this fairytale would end with my heart in shreds.

CHAPTER 18

ROURKE

The next week, on the one-month anniversary of my hire date, Nicky walked into my office, unannounced, and sat on the corner of my desk. I glanced up from Menshikov's social calendar and frowned. Nicky smiled back at me, his grin slow and lazy. By the sparkle in his gray eyes, he had mischief on his mind.

"Good afternoon, Rourke. May I call you Rourke? After all, we're old friends, right?"

"Ms. Donahue is fine." Better to set clear boundaries between us from the start. I'd been dreading this moment since the first time he'd appeared at Roman's door. Keeping my cool, I placed my pen on the desk and smiled up at him. "What can I do for you? Mr. Menshikov's on a phone call. Do you want me to let him know you're here?"

Today, he wore jeans, and a navy blazer, the throat of his ice-blue shirt open at the throat, exposing a sliver of smooth, tanned skin. "Actually, I'm here to see you. I thought maybe we could have dinner tomorrow night."

Blood thundered through my veins until I heard my heart

beating in my ears. I glanced at Roman's closed door. "I'm not sure that's a good idea."

"Why not?" With a graceful slide, he moved to my side of the desk, so close I could feel the heat of his legs on my forearm. Gooseflesh prickled along my skin. "We can pick up where we left off the night of the masquerade."

"I don't know what you're talking about." I tried to scoot my chair from the desk, but his foot lodged against the wheel, blocking my escape.

"Come on, Cinderella. Don't play that game with me. It's insulting." He picked up my pen and twirled it between his fingers, an impish smile playing on his lips. "Unlike your boss, I'm not blind to what's in front of me."

"Please." Fear thickened in my throat. "Keep your voice down." My nervous glance slid to Roman's door.

"Don't worry, love. Your secret is safe with me. I won't tell as long as you have dinner with me—tomorrow night." With slow deliberation, he placed the pen in the carousel next to my computer screen and drew my hand into his.

"That's blackmail." The touch of his lips to my hand sent an electric shiver up my back, a bizarre combination of revulsion and desire.

"I know. It's exciting, isn't it?" Over my knuckles, his eyes flashed. "Come on. Say yes. I have a table for two at Swerve." The warm puff of his breath seared my skin.

The door to Menshikov's office opened. I tried to reclaim my hand, but Nicky held fast to it.

"What's going on?" Roman's eyes narrowed. "Stop harassing the staff, Nicky."

"Am I harassing you?" Nicky asked, still holding my hand. This time, I managed to jerk it from his grasp. His chuckle brought a flush of heat into my cheeks.

"No, it's fine." I dropped my hands into my laps, afraid Nicky would blurt the truth to my boss if I protested.

"It doesn't look that way to me." A muscle ticked in Roman's cheek as his gaze caught mine and held it. We rarely looked directly at each other, but every time we did, heat and lust and restless yearning lit up my insides. "What did you need, Nicky? I've only got a minute."

"Actually, I came here to see Cin—Rourke." He corrected himself at the last minute, sending my heart into palpitations. "We're having dinner tomorrow night." Nicky lifted his thick brown brows at me. The bastard had me over a barrel, and he was enjoying it way too much.

"Really?" The way Menshikov dragged out the two syllables denoted his disapproval. It gave me a weird sense of satisfaction. Although I knew in my head that a romance between us was out of the question, my heart wanted him to be jealous.

"Eight o'clock then?" Nicky asked. When I nodded, the dimple deepened in his right cheek. "Excellent. I'll send my driver to pick you up."

Roman's chest rose and fell with a deep exhale. Sometime during the day, he'd ditched his suitcoat, unbuttoned the sleeves of his white dress shirt and pushed the sleeves up to his elbows. A gleaming Bulgari watch encircled his wrist, gold casing winking in the lights. His fingers flexed at his sides before he shrugged. "Suit yourself."

CHAPTER 19

ROMAN

*T*hat night, unable to sleep, I crept into Milada's purple-and-white bedroom. Posters of boy bands, pictures of her friends, and horse show ribbons covered the walls. One photograph caught my eye. It had been snapped at her eighth birthday party. Her broad smile and ponytails brought a lump to my throat.

I sat on the bed, beneath the ruffled canopy, and drew her pillow to my nose. It smelled like her, like bubble gum and sunshine. Hurt and frustration welled up inside me. I wanted to break something or someone. Instead, I stretched out on the bed and tried to reason away the anger.

On the desk next to the window, sat a large purple gift box. Rourke had found a matching saddle and bridle, all the rage among the horsey set, complete with gold appointments and monogrammed initials. Milada was going to be ecstatic when she saw it—if she ever came home.

Overcome by futile emotions, I sprang to my feet and stormed downstairs to the study. If I couldn't sleep, maybe I could get some work done. At the threshold, I collided with a soft, warm body. I grabbed Rourke by the biceps to keep us both from falling.

"Fucking hell," she shouted. The impact of our collision knocked a folder from her hands. Papers scattered across the floor. I choked back a laugh as she realized what she'd said and to whom she'd said it. "I apologize. You scared me. I don't usually talk like that." A red tide raced up her neck to her hairline.

"It's okay. I shouldn't have startled you. What are you doing?" Together, we gathered up the documents.

"I forgot to make copies of the reports like you'd asked." She brushed a lock of hair from her forehead. I curled my fingers, fighting the urge to do it for her. "I know you'll need them first thing."

"It could have waited." Our eyes met, and my heart did a dance. "I'm not that much of an asshole, am I?"

"Honestly, yes." She blew out a deep breath. "We both know you'd blow a gasket if these weren't on your desk first thing."

The truth stunned me into silence. I blinked and took a step back. Her lips tightened into a thin line. Until now, I'd never really cared what anyone thought of me. From the chill in her blue eyes, I'd crossed the line with her more than once. Her opinion mattered more to me than I realized.

Because I was too stubborn to apologize, I gave her a tight nod. "We can talk about it tomorrow." My gaze fell to her fuzzy pink robe and pajamas. "Are those pigs on your pants?"

"Oh, yes." Her flush deepened. She drew the edges of her robe closed and tightened the belt around her waist. "Everly gave them to me as a joke. She's—never mind." She snatched the last of the papers from my hand and scorched a path down the hall. I watched her go until she disappeared around the corner.

CHAPTER 20

ROURKE

The next morning, Ivan met me in my office at a little after nine. He dropped a folder on the desk and tapped it with two fingers. Although he still intimidated the hell out of me, our relationship had relaxed enough to call each other by our first names. Since I had to run every single visitor and appointment by him, we spent a lot of time talking on the phone and in person. Beneath his dour exterior lurked a quick wit and dry sense of humor I found refreshing after spending a day with my unsmiling boss.

"I need you to set up appointments with these women over the next few days." As always, he cut straight to the chase. "Their contact information is inside."

"Sure. Who are they?" I gathered the folder and started to open it, but he placed his hand on the top, pinning it to the desk. The midnight encounter with Roman had put me on edge. I'd tossed and turned the rest of night, bothered by the shadows beneath his eyes, and the pain in his voice.

"Mr. Menshikov doesn't have the time or opportunity to meet women, so whenever his…needs…become a priority, I find suitable companionship for him." His dark eyes met mine, unreadable. Embarrassment heated my face and neck as I processed the meaning of his words.

"They're prostitutes?" The idea of such a successful, handsome man paying for sex hit me like a fist in the gut. Then again, he worked nonstop, late into the night, and rarely left his apartment. In a warped way, it made sense, but I didn't like it.

"That's a harsh perspective." His blunt fingers smoothed down the length of his tie. "They're young women looking for financial assistance. Women who are willing to spend time with a handsome billionaire for a contracted amount of time in exchange for certain advancements in their careers."

"Sounds like prostitution to me," I said, unable to erase the irritation in my tone.

He snorted, amusement crinkling the corners of his eyes. "Nothing quite so sordid. Relationships are carefully negotiated. Mr. Menshikov doesn't like romantic entanglements. This way, everyone knows what to expect from start to finish, and everyone gets what they want." He studied my face, but I kept my expression neutral, afraid I'd give away my secrets.

"It's weird," I said with a shiver and nudged the folders to the far corner of my desk.

"Remember our conversation about discretion." It wasn't a question, but I nodded anyway.

Our discussion ended when Menshikov summoned me via the intercom. Ivan lifted a warning eyebrow. I shrugged. It wasn't my job to question my employer's life, no matter how repulsive it seemed to me. As long as he wasn't breaking the law, I didn't care. Which was a lie. Because I did care. Deep down, the thought of him with another woman gnawed at my insides. I didn't like him, but I didn't want anyone else to have him either. He belonged to me. Short-tempered, spoiled, and arrogant. I wanted all of him, flaws included.

I strode into his office, unsettled and irritated. "What?" At my sharp tone, he lifted his head and swept his gave over me. My nipples, also angry at the sight of his chiseled profile, stung as blood rushed into their tips. I crossed my arms over my chest. "Can I get you something?"

"Yes." He shoved back in his chair, spreading his knees, and regarded me thoughtfully. "I need you to pick up a couple of cases of wine for me. The order came in yesterday, and I need it today."

"Okay. Anything else?" I couldn't look at his full lips without thinking how they'd tasted and hating the thought of them on another woman.

"No, that's it." Turning in his chair, his attention returned to the computer screen. I was halfway to the door before he called out, "Is something wrong, Rose?"

After a month, he still couldn't get my name right. I grunted in exasperation but didn't turn around. "No, but my name—it's Rourke. R-o-u-r-k-e. Rourke." I couldn't be sure, but I thought I heard him chuckle as I slammed the door behind me.

On my way down the hall, I passed a young, petite blonde on her way into his office. An ice pick sliced through my chest. She smiled at me through red, glossy lips. I blinked at the blinding flash of even white teeth. He met her at the door and kissed her on the cheek. They made an amazing couple, his tall darkness next to her sunny beauty. Was she one of his contract girlfriends from the past or future? I cast a glance over my shoulder just in time to see Menshikov's arm slip around her waist. Our eyes met over the top of her head. One corner of his mouth curled up with smug satisfaction. Jealousy and frustration simmered just beneath the surface of my cool façade. In that moment, I hated him and her and most of all myself for caring.

I stabbed at the elevator button and fumed. Not only did I have to stand by and watch Roman be with other women, I had to set up his booty call appointments. How could I keep up this charade? Past experience had taught me that secrets never kept and lies always hurt. With eyes closed, I leaned against the cool metal wall of the elevator. Maybe Roman already knew that I was Cinderella. Maybe he didn't care.

Jose met me in front of the building and opened the door to the BMW. "Good afternoon, Ms. Donahue," he said with a tip of his hat.

I mustered a smile and slid onto the cool, quiet luxury of the soft leather backseat. With each passing day, I grew more and more accustomed to this decadent lifestyle. As much as I enjoyed having a personal driver and a luxurious Park Avenue apartment, I'd never sacrifice my self-respect for it. What kind of woman did something like that? Remembering the pretty blonde, I wrinkled my nose. The kind of woman in Menshikov's office.

"Jose, have you been with Mr. Menshikov very long?" I asked once he'd merged into traffic.

His eyes met mine in the rearview mirror. "About five years, give or take."

"Have you met any of his girlfriends?" I kept my tone casual and conversational.

"Some. Most of them don't last more than a few weeks." He studied my reflection. I looked away, focusing on the yellow cab next to us. "Why do you ask?"

"Oh, no reason, really. I need to set up reservations for his dates, and I thought you'd know where he likes to go." Even though the interior of the car was cool, heat rushed up my neck, all the way to my hairline. I'd never been a good liar, especially in front of people I knew.

"Yeah?" He lifted his cap to scratch his forehead. "Most of the time, they go to the Four Seasons. I'm sure he'll let you know his preferences."

"Of course." Bitterness tinted my tone, despite my best efforts. I gave him a fleeting smile then turned my attention to my phone. So, Roman took them to a hotel for dinner and, most likely, upstairs for dessert.

By the time I finished running errands, it was late evening. I unpacked the wine and crept to my apartment, hoping to avoid my arrogant, self-centered jerk of a boss. Tomorrow, I'd have to deal with his "girlfriends" and figure out a way to counter Nicky's threats.

❀

*N*icky's driver arrived at eight o'clock on the dot. I sat in the back of the Lincoln Town Car and tried to calm my nerves. Although I'd always wanted to eat at Swerve, I didn't appreciate the way he'd manipulated this date. As angry as I was at Nicky's tactics, part of me was excited to get away from work. I needed to make a life for myself, and this night provided the perfect escape from Roman.

I smoothed the fabric of my dress over my thighs and tried to breathe through the anxiety. Thanks to Christian, I had the quintessential little black dress, tight in all the right places and skimming over the wrong ones. After some coaxing, I'd returned the blond highlights to my hair and had swept it into a French twist. A black silk clutch and sky-high Louboutin's completed the outfit. It was classy without being overtly sexy—perfect for this evening.

My date met me in front of the restaurant. His gray gaze skated over my dress, lingering on my legs and the swells of my breasts. "You look good enough to eat," he said with a smile. Taking my hand, he bent and placed a kiss on each of my cheeks in a chic European manner.

"Thanks." I smiled back at him, determined to push aside work and my irritating boss. After a sleepless night, I'd decided to be pleasant but cool until I could figure out Nicky's motives. And, maybe, I could turn around this date to my advantage.

"I'm sorry I couldn't pick you up. My meeting ran late." He kept my hand in his as the maître d' led us through the restaurant to our table. "Thank you, Claude. Will you bring us a bottle of the usual?" he asked the man once we were seated.

"Do you come here a lot?" I asked. Quiet piano music hovered in the air. Muted shades of cream covered all the surfaces and furniture. Next to our table, the lights of the city twinkled on a background of black velvet.

"It's my restaurant, so yes." He pursed his lips, pleased by my wide-eyed expression. "What? Did you think I was unemployed?"

"No, of course not." In truth, I'd never given it any thought at all. "Is this your only restaurant, or do you have others?"

"I have twenty-five in the United States and another twenty overseas. I also own nightclubs and a few hotels here and there." As he spoke, he leaned back in the chair and crossed an ankle over his knee.

A team of waitstaff appeared, and our conversation ceased. One person took our order—or, more accurately, Nicky placed our orders without asking for my preferences. Two other people poured our wine into tall crystal goblets with delicate stems. I used the reprieve to gather my senses. Being around Nicky felt like anything could happen at any moment, and I needed to be prepared.

"So..." He swirled the contents of his wineglass and

watched the legs run down the glass before taking a sip. "How did you enjoy your first masquerade?"

I took a small taste before speaking, choosing my words carefully. "It was amazing. I know it wasn't your first, but did you enjoy it?"

"Oh, I thought it was very entertaining." The cock of his head reminded me of a cat watching a mouse before it pounced. "What was your favorite part?"

Heat spread across my chest and plunged up my neck. "Well, I liked all of it really. What about you?"

"The Devil's Playground."

My heart stopped then started up again. I cleared my throat, which had gone as dry as the Sahara Desert, and took a big drink of wine. Panicked thoughts raced through my head. Of course he knew about The Devil's Playground. He'd been to the masquerade many times and he was acquainted with Roman, although I hadn't quite figured out the nature of their relationship. Just because he knew of the Playground didn't mean he'd seen me there. I decided to play dumb. "Oh? What's that?"

"You know exactly what it is." The tips of his fingers traced the stem of his wineglass. His eyes met mine across the table. "I saw you there. Fucking. With him."

This revelation came at the exact same time that I took a drink of wine. I managed to avoid choking then downed the entire glass. "More," I croaked to the waiter at my elbow. He filled the glass halfway. I twirled a finger in the air. "All the way to the top, please."

"That's an expensive vintage," Nicky said, his smile widening. "But I approve. Drink up."

When I lifted my gaze, another pair of eyes met mine from their place across the room. Menshikov sat a few tables away with the pretty blonde next to him. I dabbed at my mouth with a napkin and tried to rein in my emotions. His schedule had denoted a business dinner without details. After a long exhale, I tried to unruffle my feathers. He wasn't accountable to me. I was his personal assistant, not his girl-friend. The sooner I accepted the fact, the better my life would be.

"I'm sorry. I didn't mean to upset you." By the smirk on his face, Nicky knew exactly what he was doing to me and liked it.

Roman shifted back in his chair, staring openly. I stared back. The top two buttons of his white dress shirt gaped open, exposing his throat and his bronzed skin. He'd pushed the sleeves of his jacket up to his elbows. Several leather bracelets stretched around his wrist, above the gold band of his watch.

"I'm not sure what you think you saw, but it wasn't me." To cover my anxiety, I gave Nicky my sweetest smile.

"Oh, it was you, alright." He shifted forward in the chair to rest an elbow on the table between us. His voice lowered. "Imagine my surprise to see you in that secret room, your dress shoved up around your waist, your panties on the floor, with Roman balls deep inside you." He shook his head and let out a huge sigh. "It was really quite shocking and a huge turn-on."

The heat slowly drained from my face, leaving ice in its wake. "I thought you went home."

"No. I said I was leaving." He steepled his fingertips between us. "You're upset, but I'm not sure why. That's what people do at the Playground, right? They watch or they fuck —whichever suits them best. Honestly, I never took you for a voyeur or an exhibitionist. If I'd known, I'd have taken you to that room myself." He paused to take a sip of water, observing me over the rim of his glass.

"I—I—I don't know what to say." The napkin in my lap

slid to the floor. One of the waiters retrieved it, while a second brought a new one.

"Relax. No judgment here. I just thought you should know that I know. It makes things a lot more interesting between the three of us, don't you think?" His bright smile suggested that he was quite pleased with himself. "Imagine my surprise to see my filthy Cinderella in Roman's office, working as his new assistant. And he's so self-absorbed that he hasn't even noticed."

"It does complicate things," I said, finding my voice again. The first course had arrived. We fell silent as the plates were placed in front of us. Against my will, I glanced across the room, my gaze meeting my employer's. This time, he nodded in silent greeting.

Nicky picked up the broken thread of our conversation as soon as we were alone again. "So how, exactly, did this happen? How did you find out about this job?"

"A friend referred me." Although the salad seemed delicious, I picked through the romaine and endive, my appetite obliterated. "I didn't know I'd be working for him until after I'd accepted the offer and signed all the paperwork."

"Really? That's unbelievable. A twist of fate and here we are—you, me, him."

"Yes, here we are," I replied.

"You know, he went on and on about you for weeks," he said, unfazed by my lack of enthusiasm. "How lovely you were, how soft your skin was, the way you laughed. It was pretty annoying."

"I'm sure you're exaggerating," I said, but my heart skipped a beat at the thought.

"No. Not in the slightest."

My stomach churned over the revelations of the night. The room seemed to shrink, the walls closing in on me. Using a napkin, I fanned my face. Sweat sprang up between my breasts. Menshikov frowned and lifted a finger to his chattering date, signaling for her to be quiet. Nicky continued talking. His words sounded distant, like he was speaking from the other end of a tunnel.

"Excuse me," I said, standing abruptly and turning to one of the waiters. "Where is the ladies room?" I needed a few minutes alone to get my head in the game.

The waiter pointed down the hall.

Nicky stood, his expression morphing from one of playful mischief to concern. "Are you okay?"

"Yes, I'm fine. I'll be right back." I gave him a weak smile and hustled to the restroom. With a hand on either side of the sink, I tried Everly's breathing exercises again. When that didn't work, I ran cold water over my wrists and dabbed a wet hand towel between my breasts. Slowly, my heartrate calmed.

What was Nicky playing at? He clearly had motives beyond the realm of my understanding. For a foolish second, I considered escaping through the back entrance. Running away would solve nothing. Deep inside, I enjoyed the danger, the thrill, the dirtiness. Here I was, boring Rourke, playing a game of seduction and intrigue between two sexy Russians. I ran through my options, trying to think several moves ahead, treating the situation like a chess game. The best option seemed to be one of patience. If I kept my mouth closed and my eyes open, eventually Nicky would reveal his intentions.

With my self-control restored, I pushed out of the door and met the snapping gaze of my employer as he exited the men's room.

"Hello," he said, falling into step beside me.

"Hi." My insides began a new dance, quaking at his near-ness and the familiar scent of his cologne.

"Are you okay?" His fingers found my elbow and drew me

to a halt. The touch of his skin against mine lit my senses on fire.

"Sure." I gave him a brave smile. "How's your date?"

"She's fine." His gaze searched mine, looking deeply into my eyes. I quickly erected a wall around my feelings to shut him out. "Are you sure you're alright? Nicky can be…difficult sometimes."

"Thank you for your concern, but I'm good." With a small jerk, I disconnected his grasp from my elbow.

"If you're in trouble, if you need anything, you can always ask me. You know that, right?"

I stopped and stared at him, confused by his sudden interest in my welfare. "Thanks. I appreciate it." He didn't say anything more, just nodded and returned to his table. I squared my shoulders and prepared to do battle with Nicky. He stood as I approached. Without meeting his gaze, I slid into my chair and replaced the napkin on my lap. "Did I miss anything?"

"No. Nothing at all."

"This salmon is delicious. Give my compliments to the chef."

"I will." We ate in silence for a few minutes before he set his fork alongside his plate. "I apologize for offending you. It was out of line, and I'm truly sorry."

"I don't think you're sorry at all," I replied lightly. "You've obviously got some kind of vendetta against my employer, and I'm stuck in the middle. So, let's cut to the chase. What do you want?"

"Nothing. Just the pleasure of your company." Although his words were convincing, a hint of dismay hovered around the corners of his mouth.

"I won't sleep with you." Anger sputtered beneath my calm expression. "Or spy on Menshikov."

"I didn't ask you to." He leaned across the table, drawing

my hand into his, and played with my fingers. To a casual observer, we probably appeared like lovers, but the only thing simmering between us was my indignation. "Don't pull away. He's watching us."

Against my better instincts, I froze. Yes, it was a petty thing to do, but I did it anyway. I wanted Roman to see that I wasn't a complete loser, despite his frequent reminders, and that I could handle myself. "You really hate him, don't you?"

"'Hate' is a very strong word. No, it's more like rivalry. He always wins. Everything. Every time. And for once, I'd like him to learn how it feels to lose something he wants." He tapped a finger on the back of my hand.

"Your logic has a flaw. He doesn't know who I am. And besides, he can have any woman he desires with a snap of his fingers. A random girl can't be the woman of his dreams."

"You seriously underestimate yourself, Rourke."

"I'm a realist. I know who I am and my limitations. Why would he want me when he has someone like her?" Although I hated myself for doing it, I glanced over at Roman. His date had moved to his side of the booth and was nuzzling his neck. With her lips on his earlobe and her hand on his arm, it was all too easy to picture them in bed together. The thought twisted my stomach. I dropped my fork and frowned.

"So, do we have a deal?" Nicky bit his lower lip, waiting for my answer. "You want him to pay for treating you so callously, for fucking and forgetting you, for flaunting that girl in front of you? Go out with me. We'll have some laughs, and in the meantime, Roman will have a fit. It's a win-win situation."

I didn't get a chance to answer, because the subject of our conversation strode over to our table. My gaze went directly to his hand and the blonde clinging to it. She gazed up into his face. He stared at my hand, clasped with Nicky's. If the situation had been less confusing, I would have laughed out loud at the crosscurrent of emotions. The four of us wore a multitude of hats—employer, employees, lovers, and rivals. The lines between our roles had blurred until I didn't know where I fit in anymore.

"We're leaving," Menshikov said. "You can ride home with us, Ms. Donahue."

"What?" Nicky and I said at the same time.

The nerve of this man. It was bad enough that I had to be at his beck and call every minute of every day, watch him with another woman, and know that I could never be with him in real life. Now, he demanded control of my personal life, ending my date without my permission. Even though I longed to be alone in my apartment, I wouldn't give him the satisfaction.

"Maybe she's not ready to go home," Nicky said.

Roman adjusted the lapels of his jacket. Arrogance and power oozed from every pore of his body, sharpening my attraction to him until it sliced through my chest. His stare burned through me. "I need you to pack for me. I'm flying to Miami tomorrow. Two days. Business *and* pleasure."

The faces of the people around us receded into the background. The buzz of conversation and piano music faded to silence. It was just him, me, and the lies between us. What lurked behind the navy depths of those hooded eyes?

"Okay," I said. I agreed because I wanted to prove that I didn't care about the girl on his arm—to him and to myself.

*N*icky walked outside with us. When the limo pulled to the curb, he tugged me aside, brushed the hair from my face, and kissed me. I let him do it, knowing my boss was watching, caught in the crossfire between the two men. He tasted like wine and oregano, his lips soft and plush. I dug my fingers into his shoulders to keep my balance. One of his hands found my bottom and squeezed until Menshikov cleared his throat.

"See you later," he murmured against my mouth.

Roman glared at us. Car horns and traffic sounds filled the night. He stepped aside to let me enter the car. I slid into the far seat across from his date. Her pink-tipped fingernails tapped incessantly on her phone. Roman climbed into the car and sat next to the girl. The door shut behind him, trapping us in a chamber of misconceptions and silence.

"Hi, I'm Rourke." I extended a hand to the girl as the car pulled into the street. "The personal assistant."

"Brandy," she said without looking up. The ring of her phone interrupted our introductions. She pressed it to her ear with a semi-apologetic smile. While she spoke to her friend, she twirled a strand of hair around her index finger and snapped her chewing gum.

"You never said anything about a trip to Miami," I said to the smoldering man across from me. The way he sat in the seat, all easy grace and unapologetic maleness, grated on my nerves. If only he was less attractive, less intriguing, less *everything*. I clenched my fingers, the nails cutting half-moons into my palms.

"I don't report to you, Ms. Donahue. You work for me. Or have you forgotten?" The nonchalance of his tone stuck under my skin, but the challenge in his eyes rallied my obstinacy.

"How could I forget? You made me leave my date at the restaurant. In case you weren't aware, you don't own me. In my opinion, you're the one who has forgotten his place."

"You looked like you were in distress. I was doing you a favor."

"I don't need your favors."

Although our voices remained calm and even, the air between us thickened until I couldn't breathe. His nostrils flared. The muscles in my jaw tensed. Soothing classical music floated from the car speakers, making the situation more absurd. With a smirk, he placed a hand on Brandy's thigh. His index finger traced circles on her smooth, tanned skin. I slammed my knees together against the relentless throb of need. Those hands should be on me, in *me*, not on her. Not on a girl who seemed more interested in her phone than the man beside her. Jealousy was a double-edged sword. It sliced on the way in and on the way out.

"You're insubordinate, Ms. Donahue." Heat flashed through his eyes. He was enjoying this.

"So fire me." The glib comment slipped out before I could stop it. His hand inched further up Brandy's thigh, easing beneath the hem of her short skirt. I meant every word of my threat. *Fire me and end this torture.*

"You have no idea how much I wish I could." With a sigh, his head tipped back against the headrest, but his eyes remained locked with mine. I had a quick flash of remembrance, his hands on my hips, his impatient grunts as he rammed into me over and over and over. "Maybe you should quit."

"What? And miss out on all this fun?" I crossed my arms over my chest and turned my attention to the window. Raindrops spotted the glass. In the reflection, I could see him staring at me.

The silence in the car extended to the elevator ride upstairs. Brandy ended the call with her friend and started another one with someone else. I followed them into the living room, intending to head upstairs and begin the packing process. At the foot of the stairs, Menshikov took the phone out of Britney's hands, ended her call, and pulled her in for a long kiss. She gave a little moan as his mouth opened hers, and her fingers dug into his hair.

A flush of mortification crept into my cheeks. I'd never hated anyone before, but I hated this girl. Then, I hated myself for hating her. She was an innocent bystander in this bizarre situation and had done nothing to deserve my animosity. The longer I watched their kiss, the more conflicting my feelings became. Part of my enjoyed watching them. The rest of me seethed. Jealousy and frustration mingled together. With huge effort, I peeled my eyes away from their entwined bodies and headed toward his room.

"Where are you going?" His voice, soft and dangerous, followed me.

I stopped, one hand on the railing, a foot on the next step, but didn't turn around. "To pack for you."

I made my way to the master suite and tried to ignore the

king-size four-poster bed in the middle of the room. A fire crackled in the fireplace, and the sexy purr of R&B began to pour out of the house speakers. Laughter and squeals carried through the empty house. Inside his massive walk-in closet, I dialed down the volume and rolled up my sleeves.

The closet was more like a shrine. White marble tile ran from wall to wall. I flipped on the switch for the chandelier. Recessed lighting illuminated dozens of shelves. Rows of shoes and suits and dress shirts stared back at me. The haphazard organization grated on my nerves. No one needed this many clothes.

I closed my eyes and conjured calming thoughts, but all of them involved skewering Roman Menshikov. With no information to go on, I pulled together a comprehensive wardrobe and accessories from the chaos in the closet. Two suits, dress shoes, two casual outfits, and beach wear. From the locked display case, I pulled out two pairs of diamond cuff links and their matching tie clips. After a few moments, the intricacy of the task took my mind off of whatever sexcapade was happening downstairs. Screw Roman. He might be an exiled prince, but I was a rebellious, stubborn American, and I would not be defeated.

❦

*A*n hour later, from the refuge of my bedroom, I phoned Everly and poured out the whole story—well, all of it except Nicky's blackmail. "And then he said, 'I need you to pack for me.' Can you believe the nerve of this guy?" I shouted in the phone as I stripped out of my pretty little dress. "What is wrong with this man?"

"He sounds like a jerk." As always, Everly had my back. "Why don't you quit? I'll ask around. Maybe someone has an opening for you."

"I can't quit. The money is amazing, and there's my aunt and this fantastic apartment." I flopped onto the bed and stared up into the taffeta-lined canopy. Before the masquerade, my life had been boring and predictable. Every day in Roman's employ brought a new adventure. The challenges with Roman and Nicky were more intoxicating than the best wines.

"Money and a nice home aren't everything," Everly said.

Something in her tone brought me to a sitting position. "Is everything okay?" Over the past couple of weeks, our phone calls had been brief. There were plenty of excuses for the shortage of communication. Working for her husband's company kept her busy. By the time I got off work each night, I was too exhausted for more than a quick text. Phone conversations and Facetime eased the pain of separation, but in moments like these, I needed to be in the same room with her. I missed the subtle cues of body language and facial expressions.

"Of course." She laughed, and the tightness in my chest lessened. As long as she retained her sense of humor, things couldn't be too bad. "I'm just saying there's more to life than those things."

"Who is this? Put Everly back on the phone," I demanded, only half teasing. As a woman of power, wealth, and privilege, statements like that were uncharacteristic.

"Stop. You know what I mean."

"I know." I rolled onto my stomach and stared out the window at the darkness. Lightning flashed in the distance. The rumble of thunder followed a few seconds later.

"I'm coming home next month for my cousin's wedding. Promise me you'll take some time off so we can hang together."

"Sure. Text me the dates so I can put in a vacation

request." My cell phone rang with an incoming call. "Hang on. Satan is calling." I picked up the second phone. "Hello?"

"Hey. I need you to run to the drug store and pick up condoms." Roman's deep voice reverberated through my ear. My jaw slackened. The coil of jealousy in my belly, the one that had started this afternoon, tightened to the point of pain.

"Excuse me?" I asked. On the other phone, Everly broke into peals of laughter. I lifted it to my ear, muting Roman's call. "Everly, hush. He can hear you. I'll call you later."

"Okay. Love you," she said.

"Love you," I replied, and unmuted Menshikov's phone.

"I had no idea you felt so strongly about me." His amusement transferred over the air waves. I slapped a hand against my forehead. This day had been a disaster since the moment I'd opened my eyes this morning. Nothing could make it any worse.

"Oh, I definitely feel strongly," I said through gritted teeth. "But I don't think love is the proper name for it."

"Who were you talking to? Do you have company?"

"You know I'm alone. You forced me to leave my date to pack for a trip that you failed to inform me about." The hasty words hung in the air. During my career as a personal assistant, professionalism had been my number-one priority. Even though Everly was my best friend, we maintained a healthy balance between work and friendship. Menshikov possessed the ability to strip away my defenses. I drew in a deep breath and tried to center myself. "I apologize. That was out of line."

"Yes, it was." Why did I get the feeling he was laughing at me? "We're wasting time here, Rochelle."

"Rourke. My name is Rourke. If I'm going to buy you condoms, the least you can do is get my name right." The dial tone buzzed in my ear. The bastard had hung up on me.

Fuming, I called his driver and pulled on a pair of sweats and a T-shirt. What kind of jerk sent his assistant to buy condoms in the middle of the night? The thought of him with that girl, his heavy body on hers, her legs wrapped around his waist, topped off my jealousy. Hair askew, I stormed down to the lobby.

The driver double-parked in front of the store. I ran down the sidewalk, splashing through puddles. From the drug store, I called Menshikov, hoping to disturb his night the way he'd disturbed mine. He answered on the fourth ring.

"What kind?" I asked.

"Sorry?" His voice was rough, sleepy.

"Brand? Size? Lubricated? Ribbed?" My words came out choppy and dripping with animosity, but at this point, I didn't care. "Glow-in-the-dark? Flavored? Latex?"

"Um, just bring a variety. Magnum." He hung up again.

Thirty minutes later, I trudged up the stairs to his room and pounded on the door. Water dripped from my hair and puddled on the tile floor. I was soaked to my underwear. After a few seconds, he opened the door, wearing a pair of silk boxers, rumpled hair, and a smirk. I'd never seen him without a shirt before. Black hair dusted his chest and blazed a dark trail beneath the waistband of his underwear. Lines of muscle and sinew rippled down his torso.

"Took you long enough," he said. The width of his broad shoulders blocked the room. Not that I wanted to see anything. Just knowing the girl was in there, nestled in the twisted sheets of his bed, made my insides glow. His gaze ran up and down my drenched body.

"You're welcome." I shoved the bag of condoms into his outstretched hand.

"You're dripping on my floor."

"Really? I hadn't noticed." I turned and strode in the

direction of my apartment. Letting my attitude show in the swing of my hips.

"Aren't you going to clean that up?" he called after me.

"Nope." *Score one, Rourke Donahue.*

"You really shouldn't wear white in the rain." His chuckle followed me down the hall.

I glanced down at my chest. In my haste, I'd thrown on a white T-shirt and skipped the bra. Soaked cotton clung to the swells of my breasts, nipples clearly visible through the sheer fabric.

"Crap," I muttered beneath my breath. No wonder the guy at the drug store had ogled me.

Inside my bathroom, I stripped off the sopping clothes and tossed them into the sink. Never, in all my days, had I been so humiliated, angry, turned on, and confused. Part of me wanted to hate him, and part of me loved the way he challenged me at every turn. Before going to sleep, I vowed to bring this man to his knees one way or another.

"Game on," I muttered and turned out the lights.

CHAPTER 22

ROMAN

ive-thirty in the morning rolled around way too quickly. I awoke with a terrible thirst and a vague sense of shame over my behavior. Last night had been a fiasco of epic proportions. For the first time in years, I hit snooze on the alarm clock and went back to sleep, unable to face the consequences of my actions or another day without my daughter.

When the alarm went off for the second time, I rolled out of bed and into the shower. Soap and hot water failed to wash away the embarrassment. I'd been a total ass to Rourke last night. The site of her with Nicky had boiled my blood, and I'd lost my common sense. When he'd kissed her on the sidewalk, I'd lost my mind, as well. I'd forced her to pack for a nonexistent trip, but it had been the only excuse I could think of to get her out of his arms. Then I'd sent her out in the rain to buy condoms for a girl I'd had no intention of fucking. All to satisfy my need to protect her from my little brother and to prove that I was in control.

Except I wasn't in control. If anything, I'd come out a loser in the game. I'd gone to bed alone—again—like I had every night since the masquerade. Brandy had tried her best to persuade me otherwise. Despite her efforts, I couldn't get past the thought of Nicky's hands on Rourke's ass or the way her lips had been red and bee-stung in the limo from his kiss.

The women of my past had never created anything more than a lust that waned as quickly as it appeared. My curvaceous assistant, however, had managed to do both. I enjoyed her smart mouth and efficiency almost as much as I loved to torment her. The fire in her eyes set spark to feelings I'd thought long dead, emotions killed by Milada's mother and the women who'd come after her. I was totally and completely obsessed with Rourke. Hell, it seemed, had frozen over.

"Good morning." Ivan fell into step with me as I passed through the hall and headed toward the study. "You're looking like a ray of sunshine today."

Rourke stood outside my office door, arms crossed over her chest. The storm cloud over her head mimicked the weather outside.

"And so does Ms. Donahue," Ivan continued. "Have you two had a lovers' spat?"

Sometimes Ivan's dry sense of humor prickled under my skin. I shot him a murderous glare and ignored the question. "Any news on Milada?"

The gleam in his eyes diminished. "One of our contacts spotted them at the airport in Barbados. Apparently, they left by private plane. We've been unable to confirm their destination."

"Oh." The news turned my blood to ice. I shoved a hand through my hair, thinking in the back of my mind that I needed a haircut. Three months since Milada had gone missing, and each day had been like a knife blade to my heart. "What's our next move?"

By now, we'd reached Rourke. She opened the door for us

and followed on our heels. Irritation rolled off her in waves. Ivan gave her a speculative glance. She had her hair piled on top her head, and new, sexy librarian glasses perched on her nose. The angrier she became with me, the more I wanted to throw her over my knee and give that round ass a few smart spanks.

"It's okay to talk in front of her," I told Ivan. Throughout our battles, I'd come to respect her tenacity and work ethic. No matter how much she hated me, she'd never violated my trust. Not once. Trustworthy employees in my world were worth their weight in gold.

"I think we should put some pressure on your ex. If you cut off her allowance and credit cards, she'll come running," Ivan said.

"I hate to do that. You know the one who will suffer is Milada." For the millionth time, I cursed myself for hooking up with a money-sucking vampire. I'd been young and dumb and full of cum when we met, and I'd been paying for my mistake ever since.

"I don't think you have any choice," Ivan replied.

Rourke poured coffee and brought it to my desk. As always, she'd laid out pertinent news stories from the day, but my schedule was absent.

I shuffled through the pages. "Where's my itinerary?"

"I didn't print your itinerary, because you're flying to Miami today." Her mouth pinched into a tight rosebud. "If you'd informed me about the trip in a timely manner, I'd have been able to make adjustments to your schedule and have one ready."

Once Ivan had given me the news about Milada, I'd forgotten about the Miami lie and all the ways I'd shown my ass last night. I stifled a sigh of irritation at myself and stared her in the eyes, daring her to remark. "Right. Trip's canceled."

Those eyes deserved poems and flowers and songs to be

written in their honor. Some days they were pale blue. On other days, like today, they were more gray and churned like a turbulent sea. She blinked, anger simmering just below the surface, and exhaled. "Good to know."

"Is that a problem?" I asked.

"No. Of course not." One blink of those lacy lashes, and her expression changed from one of annoyance to amusement. "It's what you pay me for. I'll print out your schedule right away. Is there anything else I can do for you? Lick your stamps?"

"I'd like you to inventory all my clothes and organize my closet. Someone left it in a mess last night. Think you can get that done today?" It was a bullshit project, but one I'd been thinking about for a while. There was no way she could complete it in a single afternoon. At least, this way, she'd be busy, and I'd know where she was.

Blood climbed from the open throat of her blouse, up her slender neck, and settled in her cheeks. "There's nothing I'd rather do." Sweetness and complicity filled her tone, but those goddamn eyes flashed. What I wouldn't give to turn her over my knee and give her a good spanking. Something about her incited the devil inside me. I wanted to tame her, claim her, and bend her stubborn will to meet mine.

"Are you done bickering?" One of Ivan's thick black brows arched. By the curl of his lips, he enjoyed the display between us.

"Continue." I twirled a finger through the air.

He scrolled through the messages on his phone. "It looks like she just bought lunch at a restaurant in London. I can have someone in the area within the hour."

"Then why are you standing here?" I snapped, my concerns immediately going back to my daughter.

"On it, sir." Ivan gave a small bow and disappeared on silent feet.

I buried my head in my hands and groaned. For the last three months, I'd been patient, controlled, and calm. News of their sightings came in, one after the other, sometimes all at once, and sometimes not at all. Through these reports, I'd held my breath, hoping each one would be the break necessary to bring Milada home. And each time, I'd been wrong. We were always a day too late or a city behind.

Through my fingers, I watched low-heeled pumps cross the carpet and stop in front of my feet. My gaze traveled up slender calves, past the hem of her blue dress and the belt wrapped around a narrow waist, over her full breasts and stopped on her face.

"I'm sorry," she said softly and placed a gentle hand on my shoulder. The warmth of her fingertips sent a shockwave down my arm. "You must love her very much."

"Yes." The broken admission rasped past the thickness in my throat.

"I can't imagine how difficult this must be for you. Is there anything I can do to help?" The sincerity in her tone placed a crack in the shield around my emotions. A lot of years had passed since any woman had touched me with more than lust.

"No."

She hovered at my feet for a few beats.

Apologize, Roman. I opened my mouth, but nothing came out. Contrition had never been my one of my strong suits. A man in my position never had to apologize for anything. At least, that was what I'd been told. We stared at each other, the seconds passing, my heart beating faster. If only she knew what I knew, we wouldn't be having this stupid conversation. She'd be kneeling at my feet, and I'd take control of that sweet, sassy mouth.

"Well, I'll get to work then." With a nod, she left the room and closed the door behind her.

For the rest of the day, I threw myself into work. Because it was a Saturday, I spent the day in my study, tying up loose ends from the previous week and devising strategies for the future. Under normal circumstances, this was my favorite day, a day for lounging in sweat pants, catching up on news, watching baseball. Today, however, I couldn't shake the worry over Milada. No matter how many reports I read, how many phone calls I made, her innocent, round face hovered in front of my eyes.

Unable to stand the sensation of powerlessness, I phoned Ivan. "Any news?"

"They were definitely in London." The quiet, noncommittal undertone in his voice sent a chill down my back.

"But they're not now?" I shifted back from the desk and closed my eyes, willing him to say the words I wanted to hear.

"We think it was just a long layover. It's a possibility they moved out of the country. We're checking the leads now."

I hung up the phone then walked to the window and stared over the bustling city. In another week, Milada would have her twelfth birthday, and I wouldn't be there to celebrate with her. If I knew her mother at all, she'd used the time to fill our daughter's head with lies and misinformation, to turn her against me. With a sigh, I rested a palm against the glass and concentrated on the line of traffic crawling its way up Park Avenue.

"Plotting world domination?" Nicky's sarcastic question slammed the door shut on my thoughts. He sauntered into the room in his cocky, playful way.

"What is it, Nicky?" Given the circumstances, I didn't have the patience for his mischief. "I've seen more of you in the last month than the past five years. What are you up to?"

"No 'Hello'? 'How are you?' You really need to work on your social skills." Resting a hip on the corner of my desk, he toyed with the stapler. I took it from his hands and returned it to its place.

"Hello. How are you?" I asked to humor him.

"Well, I'm a little pissed off about your behavior last night. Thank you for asking."

We'd played these games for the majority of our lives. When we were kids, Nicky had been the annoying younger kid, always tugging on my shirtsleeve. As teenagers, we'd competed against each other for everything: sports, cars, women. Once Claudette had come along and she'd become pregnant, the game had lost its luster for me, because now I had a child to consider, one who didn't deserve to be manipulated. Nicky, however, couldn't stop.

"From now on, Rourke is off limits." Ending the conversation, I powered up the computer.

"I don't think so." Despite my dirty looks, he didn't move from the desk. "I like her, and I think she likes me too. She might be the one."

I stared at him for a minute then burst into laughter. "Don't be ridiculous."

"Am I?" With his hair tousled by the wind, he looked like a young boy again. He stood and wandered to the new abstract mounted over the sofa, clasped his hands behind his back, and stared at the swirls of color. "If your ego wasn't so enormous, you'd be able to see how crazy she is about me. We've been sneaking around for weeks, stealing precious moments together. She's worried you won't understand."

Although I pretended to be unruffled by his comment, my guts clenched at the thought of her in any man's arms, let alone his. "Go home, Nicky. I have work to do."

"Suit yourself, but next time you ruin my date, I won't be so nice about it."

The pressure of work, worry for Milada, and sexual frustration culminated in a growl from my throat. I stood and slapped both hands on the desk. "Do not come in here and threaten me. I'm not playing your stupid games any longer. Rourke isn't some prize. She's a real person. Haven't we hurt enough people? Leave her alone."

Stunned by my outburst, he stared, wide-eyed, until Rourke knocked on the frame of the open door. "Excuse me, but is everything okay? I can hear you all the way into the kitchen."

In unison, my brother and I turned to face her. With her hair in a ponytail and minus cosmetics, she looked much younger than twenty-six. Tight running pants hugged her hips and thighs, but my gaze stuttered over the strip of bare skin between her waistband and running bra.

"Hi, babe," Nicky closed in and bent to give her a kiss, but she turned her head at the last minute. His lips grazed her cheek instead. I choked back a chuckle.

"Good morning." The greeting was for him, but her eyes found mine and held there. A curious flutter twisted my stomach, pleasant yet unnerving.

"What's up?" I asked.

"I'm going for a run on my lunch hour, unless you need something right away. I've got to work off some of the weight I've gained." At her words, my gaze involuntarily slid over her full breasts and the curves further down. In my opinion, she was perfect.

"You're welcome to use my gym," I said. Nicky's gaze flitted from me to her then back again, confusion furrowing his brow. No one was allowed to use my private workout facilities, not even him. "On your downtime, of course."

"Thanks, but I wouldn't want to impose." She shifted from one foot to the other. Maybe she sensed the tension between me and my brother. Or maybe it was the sexual tension that stretched taut as a guitar string between us. My eyes kept bouncing from her lips to her breasts, despite my best efforts to keep them under control.

"It's not an imposition."

"I wish you'd told me you were going for a run. I'd have joined you," Nicky said, stepping into my line of sight, breaking the visual connection between me and Rourke.

I laughed. "You haven't worked out a day in your life." His murderous glare tickled my funny bone even more. I lifted an eyebrow, daring him to deny it. "The guy owns a chain of workout facilities and has never set foot in one, ever."

"That's not true. I went to one in Las Vegas—once. Granted, it was by accident. My GPS gave the wrong directions. I was actually looking for the bar next door, but I think that counts. Don't you?" When Nicky wanted, he possessed more charisma than anyone I'd ever met. He ramped up the charm for Rourke, showing his dimples. She smiled, and suddenly, the humor dissipated from the conversation.

"What about the closet?" As soon as the question rolled off my tongue, her smile turned into a frown. It was a dick move, but jealousy removed the filter between my thoughts and my mouth.

"I'm not even going to dignify that with an answer." The tip of her nose tilted higher. "I'll be back in thirty minutes."

"God, you're an ass." Nicky's laughter made the tips of my ears burn with irritation. "No wonder you can't find a girlfriend." He winked at Rourke, and they shared another grin, escalating my embarrassment. Outside, the sun moved behind a cloud and shadowed the city.

"It's okay. He can't help himself." The muscle beneath her cheek twitched, underlining her disapproval. "I'm used to it."

I didn't want to admit Nicky was right, but I *was* an ass. Too many years as a spoiled, overentitled, megalomaniac had ruined me for polite company. In desperation, I floundered for a way to gain her approval. A photo of my new yacht flashed across the screensaver on my computer display. "When you get a minute, I'd like to get your input on décor for my yacht."

"You have a yacht?" She bit her lower lip, eyebrows raising. "Everly's father had one—a small one. We used to go out on weekends sometimes. I really enjoyed it."

"It's being delivered next week. I'll need you to go with me to inspect it." I made a mental note to remember this tidbit for later. "Maybe we can take it for a spin around the harbor."

"Yes, that would be awesome." There it was, the smile I'd been yearning for, and all for me. I smirked at my brother, reveling in his scowl. Then her smile faded, like the sunshine on the New York horizon. "Do I need to stock it with condoms?"

"Come along, Rourke. I'll walk you downstairs," Nicky said, wrapping his fingers around her elbow, and shot a smile of pure delight over his shoulder.

I crumpled the piece of paper in my hand and watched them disappear through the door. Emptiness gnawed my gut as I reclaimed my seat behind the desk. Despite the size of my bank account, I couldn't buy the skills to seduce a woman like Rourke. We'd gotten off on the wrong foot, and I had no idea how to get back in her good graces.

CHAPTER 23

ROURKE

A few minutes after eight that evening, Roman called. I gritted my teeth at the familiar ringtone. "I need to see you in my room. Now."

The steely edge to his request made my stomach flip. The entire day had been spent sorting through his clothes, photographing each item, and entering its picture plus description into an iPad. I'd recruited one of the housemaids to assist. While I manipulated the data, she'd arranged the clothing according to season, color, and purpose. We'd finished a few minutes ago, and I was in the process of running hot water into the tub for a relaxing bath when he called. After a sigh of resignation, I shut off the taps, pulled on a bathrobe, and padded through the silent house.

Outside Menshikov's room, I rapped on the door and pressed my sweaty palms together. Heaven knew what his request might be. More condoms. A triple chocolate shake from the ice cream joint down the street. The longer I waited, the greater my irritation became. The man had no boundaries. Maybe it was time for me to show him mine.

The door opened. I bit my lower lip and tried not to stare at his bare chest, the long lines of his torso, or the ripples of abdominal muscles above his silk boxers. Our eyes met, and I got lost in the churning depths of his irises. Inky-black hair spilled over his forehead. It took all my self-control to keep from slipping my fingers through those glossy strands and pushing them away from his face.

"Explain." He strode toward the closet, his tight ass bunching and flexing beneath the fabric of his boxers. With an angry jerk, he flung the door open. "What is this?"

"Um, your closet." My temper simmered. Following Nicky's visit, we'd been tiptoeing around each other all day. An argument loomed on our horizon. I was done taking crap from him, and by the flash of his eyes, something itched beneath his skin, too.

"I can't find a damn thing." His full lips tightened into a grim line. His bare feet slapped against the tile as he paced along the shelves of footwear.

"What are you looking for?" A chuckle tickled the back of my throat. I coughed to keep it from escaping.

"Pajamas."

"They're here." I tapped the second drawer of the center island. "All of your underwear, socks, and incidentals are in these drawers, grouped by color and purpose." Nudging him aside, I pointed to the iPad on the island countertop and swiped a finger across the display. "An inventory of your clothing is here. I've contacted your stylist. She'll be able to update your wardrobe with new purchases."

He stared at me, nostrils flaring, the epitome of every sexual fantasy I'd ever possessed. "When I asked you to organize my closet, I meant put things in order, not screw it all up."

I glanced around the pristine room. Gleaming-white cabinets, sparkling mirrors, and marble countertops shone back at me. Everything was perfect, down to the fresh centerpiece of white roses and ivy on the island. I crossed my arms over my chest. "No."

"No?" He mimicked my pose and arched a thick black eyebrow. The veins stood out on his flexing biceps. Apparently, he'd never heard the word before.

"No, you do not get to berate me for doing an excellent job. I went above and beyond here. This is perfection." I lifted my chin and dared him to challenge me.

He took a step closer until the tips of his bare feet brushed my socks. When his chest rose and fell with an exasperated breath, an ache spread through my breasts and down the insides of my thighs. The scent of his cologne filled my nose. I wanted to run my hands over his smooth, bare skin and down the curve of his back. The tilt of his chest brought his nose within an inch of mine.

"I asked you to organize it, not reconfigure the whole thing." His eyes were dark, deep, infinite like the ocean, and surrounded by long, black lashes. Their focus dipped to my lips. "If I wanted you to deconstruct it, I'd have asked you."

"You know this is a great job," I said, keeping my voice low and even, while my insides quaked with lust and fury. "If you don't like it, maybe next time you'll be more specific."

"I shouldn't have to be specific. You should know what I want."

"That's the most insane thing I've ever heard. I'm not a mind reader."

A knock on the door broke us apart. Roman shoved past me and opened the door. Ivan swept in. Rain dotted the lapels of his black suit. His gaze swept over my employer's bare chest and my bath robe. A flicker of amusement crossed his face then disappeared.

"I just wanted to let you know we've located your daughter," Ivan said. Roman stopped breathing. "They just crossed the border into the Ukraine."

"What?" The air vibrated with the strength of Roman's frustration. "How did this happen?"

"They slipped past our guy and through customs before he could do anything." Sincere remorse shadowed Ivan's sharp features.

"Tell me she's okay." Roman's voice broken on the last word. This rare show of emotion reminded me of the man lurking beneath his tailored suits and persona of power, someone vulnerable and sensitive.

"My contact says she looked healthy but tired. We won't give up. I'm searching now for someone to enter the country on our behalf. Hell, I'll go myself if I have to." Ivan shook his head and stared at the floor. "I'm so sorry, Roman."

Menshikov placed a hand on his shoulder and squeezed. "It's okay. You've done everything you can. Just stay on it, would you?"

"Of course." With a deep inhale, Ivan squared his shoulders, his implacable facade sliding over his face again. "I'll never give up."

I stood rooted to the floor until Ivan's back disappeared into the hallway. Menshikov ran a hand through his hair, paced the floor twice, then picked up the scented candle I'd bought for his nightstand and chucked it against the wall. The glass holder shattered into a thousand pieces. The heavy weight of the piece dented the drywall, something I'd have to get repaired in the morning.

"Is there anything I can do?" I twisted my hands helplessly. The pain on his face squeezed my chest, his distress palpable. "Do want to talk? Or can I get you a drink—scotch or vodka?"

"No. Just…just leave me." He sank onto the edge of the bed, cradling his head in his hands, and I left the room with an ache between my ribs. The pain in his eyes resonated with me. I understood how it felt to lose someone you loved.

꧁꧂

*T*wo hours later, I stared at the ceiling from my bed. The soft sheets rustled in the quiet. Roman had everything—everything but the one thing he wanted. No amount of power or wealth or good looks could help him in this situation. What made his ex so angry that she'd kept his daughter away from him? Men like him didn't come into wealth and power without some dirty skeletons in their closets. I snorted, thinking of his temper tantrums and his arrogance. Despite his shortcomings, the pain in his eyes suggested caring and love, adding another layer to this complicated man.

His ringtone shattered the silence. I groaned, rolled onto my stomach and placed the pillow over my head. Even though he'd be furious, I let the call go to voicemail—twice. This man's irritability and beauty had tormented me enough for one day. Five minutes later, someone rapped on the front door. I jumped out of bed, fuming, and stomped to answer the incessant pounding.

"If you got me out of bed for anything less than a building fire, I'm going to be seriously pissed." I yanked the door open and came face to face with my employer. Roman stood in the hallway, looking rumpled and out of sorts. The open edges of his silk robe fluttered as he pushed past me and into the living room. The faint odor of cologne and liquor floated in his wake. I rolled my eyes. "You can't just storm into my place uninvited."

"If you didn't want me in here, you shouldn't have

answered the door." He strode into the living room and turned to face me.

"What do you want?" I closed the door and leaned against the frame. "Wait. Don't tell me. You've shagged your way through all those condoms, and you need more."

One corner of his mouth twitched. "No. I'm good. Thanks for asking." His curious dark eyes scanned the room. "This is a nice place. Small though."

"You've never been in here before?"

"No. Why would I be?"

"I don't know. Pestering your assistants, maybe?"

"Humph." Long fingertips skimmed the edge of the sofa back. With his demeanor softened by vodka and his hair tousled, he looked younger but no less approachable. "None of the others stayed long enough to be pestered."

"Maybe if you remembered their names and didn't yell so much, they'd stick around longer."

"You've stuck around. My yelling doesn't seem to bother you." To my great consternation, he wandered across the room to look at the picture of my aunt on the fireplace mantle. "Who's this?"

"It's my aunt May. If you don't mind, I'd like to get back to sleep."

"The one who raised you?" The past month had been busy, but I didn't remember telling him about her. A slow warmth spread across my skin. His acknowledgement of such a personal detail set my expectations on their ear.

"Yes." Instead of returning to the couch, he padded on bare feet into the kitchen and began rummaging through the refrigerator. I trotted after him, wishing I'd grabbed my robe to cover my tiny tank top and braless chest. "What are you looking for?"

"Can I have some water?"

"Sure." His nearness doubled my heartrate. I found a glass and filled it with water from the tap. Our forearms brushed. He was too close, drowning my kitchen with his soap-and-vodka scent. "I don't have any bottled water. This will have to do."

"Why not? Isn't Drenda doing her job?" He braced a hand on the cabinet behind me, boxing me in, the same way he'd done at the masquerade. The strength ebbed from my knees. "I'll talk to her tomorrow."

"It's fine. I can do my own shopping." I slipped beneath his arm and handed the glass to him.

"No. It's not. I want you free in case I need anything." In two gulps, he drained the glass. I watched the play of muscles in his throat. Somehow, he managed to make something as mundane as drinking look sexy. It was so unfair. He set the glass on the edge of the sink then walked back to the living room and straight toward my bedroom.

"Mr. Menshikov, it's late, and I—"

"Call me Roman."

"Okay," I rubbed my palms over my thighs and tried again. "What can I do for you, Roman?"

"I'm sorry for yelling at you. The closet looks great." By now he stood in the center of my bedroom, making me wish I'd picked up the dirty laundry on the floor and tidied the bed. The sight of him in my most private room made me think about him in my bed with those one-thousand-thread-count sheets tangled around his naked hips. "I was upset about Milada. You did a good job."

"And?" I tried not to show my surprise and arched an eyebrow.

"You're supposed to say thank you."

"Thank you." After undressing for bed, I'd thrown my bra haphazardly aside. He stared at the lacy cups dangling in front of him. I snatched it from the footboard and shoved it into a dresser drawer. "What about interrupting my date with Nicky?"

"I won't apologize for that," he said with a slow shake of his head. His focus traveled along the rumpled bedsheets to the headboard. My gaze followed his. The white-and-gold mask from the masquerade winked in the low light. I held my breath, waiting, while he studied it. "You'd be smart to stay away from him."

"You're my employer. You have no say in my personal life, especially who I date." Anxiety fluttered in my belly as he fingered the edge of the mask. It was one of a kind, hand-made, and unmistakable. "If this...relationship...is going to work, we need to set some boundaries."

"True." He dropped his hand to his side and turned to face me, his gaze connecting with mine. Mystery and intrigue swirled behind those dark eyes. Did he know who I really was? Was this part of the game between him and Nicky? "But I believe there's a non-fraternization clause in your employment contract, forbidding you to date members of my family. And Nicky, you see, is my younger brother."

"I—I didn't know that. Why didn't you tell me?" Random clips of the two men rolled through my head. They were nothing alike in physical appearance or mannerisms. Even their surnames differed. "How was I supposed to know?"

"His father adopted me. I assumed Nicky would have told you, since you're so close." Did I imagine a hint of jealousy in his tone? The idea pleased me more than I wanted to admit.

"We're not close." The trembling of my hands echoed the quake of my insides. "I hardly know him."

"That's not what he says. According to him, you've been sneaking around behind my back for weeks. Is that true, Rourke?" The sound of my name on his lips, in his smooth voice, brought immediate dampness to my panties.

"I don't sneak around. Not with Nicky. Not with anyone."

I swallowed against the dryness in my mouth. Moonlight streamed through the window, casting the planes and angles of his face in sharp relief. There he was, my prince, my boss, the bane of my existence. "Are you going to fire me?"

"You're the best assistant I've had in years." His words of praise heated my cheeks. Soft footfalls marked his progress across the room. He stopped in front of me and drew in a deep breath through his nose, like he was scenting me. I swayed toward him and caught myself. His eyes crinkled at the corners. "It occurred to me that his fascination with you could work to my advantage." The pads of his fingers grazed my neck as he pushed a strand of loose hair over my shoulder. I wanted him to keep going, to run that elegant hand down my back, to pull me against his hard chest.

"He's blackmailing me," I blurted. Roman froze, eyes narrowing. "He—he knows something about me, and he's been threatening to tell you if I don't play along with his game."

Memories of our tryst pulled me toward him. Reflections of that night danced in the blackness of his pupils. His gaze dipped to my lips. My breath caught and held as his fingertips lifted to my face and stroked my cheek. Desire fizzed beneath my skin, popping like tiny champagne bubbles.

"Take away his power over you. Tell me your secrets, Rourke, and I'll tell you mine." The seductive murmur resonated into my core. He closed his eyes and ran the tip of his nose along the length of mine. The warmth of his breath puffed against my lips. If I angled my head the tiniest bit, our mouths would meet, and I wanted it. I wanted it more than anything, to taste him again, to feel the slide of his tongue in my mouth. When his hand fisted in the hair at the nape of my neck, I whimpered. Delicious pain skated over my scalp as he tugged my head back, exposing the vulnerable artery beneath my jaw, like he was a vampire about to take a bite.

"That night at the masquerade, it was me," I whispered.

His lips paused at the place where my pulse fluttered butterfly wings above my collarbone. The tip of his tongue licked up to the ticklish spot behind my ear. I shivered. He placed the gentlest of kisses on my earlobe and whispered, "I know."

CHAPTER 24

ROURKE

$\mathcal{R}$oman's confession robbed the strength from my knees. The place on my neck where he'd kissed me burned like I'd been branded. I sank onto the edge of the bed and stared at him. A hint of amusement curled his lips. "What do you mean?" My voice sounded strange, hollow, like it belonged to someone else.

"I know who you are, Cinderella. I've known for a while now." From his greater height, he stared down at me. "Since you picked me up at the airport."

All this time? "So what happens now?"

"Well…" Those long-lashed blue eyes dragged over my body, over the outline of my nipples poking through my tank top, and stopped at the tiny shorts hiding my sex. "I'm going upstairs to bed." On silent feet, he turned and padded toward the door.

I jogged after him. "No, I mean tomorrow. How is this going to work?"

At the front door, he turned so quickly that I stumbled backward and fell into the wall. His strong arms caged me in, one hand placed on each side of my head. The weight of his body pinned me to the plaster. Warm, full lips pressed against mine. His tongue slipped into my mouth. He tasted of vodka, mint, and a hint of lime. A growl reverberated deep in his chest. I dug my fingers into his biceps. How many nights had I dreamed of this moment, of discovering my Prince Charming, of being kissed within an inch of my life?

Heat and wetness and friction consumed my thoughts. He plundered my mouth. Male possession crushed my lips and stole my breath. One of his hands dropped to my hip and squeezed. Through the silk of his pajama bottoms, the hard length of his cock nudged my stomach. I moaned, the sound foreign and feral. If only I could get closer to him. I wanted to feel his bare flesh sliding over mine. The barriers of cotton and silk weighed heavier than iron chains.

"Easy, princess," he murmured and pulled away. Instinctively, I followed the direction of his movement. Too many sensations crowded my consciousness—the scent of his freshly showered skin, the hardness of his chest against my breasts, the silken strands of his hair in my fingers. He placed a hand on my chest and gently pushed me against the wall. I stared at him, wide-eyed and shocked. Things were happening too quickly for my overtaxed brain to process.

"Please." It was the only word I could speak with my sex throbbing and his red lips inches from mine.

He placed a fingertip beneath my chin and tilted my face so I had to look into his eyes. They were dark, almost black, his pupils dilated, obscuring the blue of his irises. With a slow shake of his head, he backed away. The air chilled between us. "Not now. Not tonight."

The door shut behind him. Alone in the living room, I stared at the door, willing him to come back and make this torturous need disappear. Questions raced around my head until I grew dizzy. How had he known it was me? Did Nicky know that he knew? The answers wouldn't come easily and as he'd said, not tonight.

※

*I*n the morning, I took particular care with my outfit, choosing a slim navy pencil skirt and a silver ruffled blouse, paired with ridiculously cute silver sandals. Inside Roman's study, bright sunshine poured through the enormous windows. I arranged everything the way I knew he liked it. Hot coffee ready and waiting. Schedule printed and emailed to his phone. He had an early meeting on the far side of the city, which would require a long car ride for the two of us. Butterflies bounced around my stomach as I waited for him to appear.

After a long and sleepless night, I'd decided to be cool and professional. While I grazed the internet for news clips, I adjusted the collar of my shirt for the third time. My neck still sizzled where his lips had touched. One tiny confession had changed everything about our relationship, both personally and professionally. I had no idea what to expect from him this morning.

At six-thirty, he walked into the study. As always, the crisp lines of his suit hugged his broad shoulders and narrow waist. I made a mental note to thank his tailor for a job well done. Sunlight glinted off the diamond-encrusted bar holding his red tie in place. He strode past me, taking the cup of coffee from my hands, and claimed his throne behind the desk. I drank in the spicy scent of his aftershave.

His blue eyes went straight to his computer display. "Anything special on the schedule today?"

"Yes." I pressed my palms together to calm their trembling. "I've got to leave a few minutes early tonight to see my aunt. She's having some problems at the nursing home, and I want to check on her."

"Done." Strong fingers tapped on the keyboard. Even his wrists turned me on, the square width of his hands, those neatly manicured nails. "What else?"

"Um, Ivan asked me to schedule some interviews for you this week." The cadence of his typing faltered, and he stilled. My blood turned to acid at the thought of him with the women in the folders.

"What about them?" The soft, deadly tone of his deep voice raised my internal temperature a dozen degrees.

"I just wanted to make sure you were aware." Of course he meant to continue with his life. Just because we'd shared hot, dirty, anonymous sex four months ago didn't mean he had an obligation to me. He was my employer. I was his assistant. Nothing had changed, and everything had changed. "You have three appointments tomorrow and Thursday."

"Cancel them," he said after a long pause. Confusion tempered the excitement at his command. What did that mean? Had last night changed his mind about the women, or was this simply a result of his busy agenda? He resumed typing. "That'll be all, Ms. Donahue."

"Right." With my heart jumping between my ribs, I walked to the doorway but stopped before leaving and returned to his desk.

"Is there something else?" With an exasperated sigh, he pushed away from the desk and looked me straight in the eyes. Flecks of gold sparked in his irises.

"Yes. I—I mean, shouldn't we talk about last night? About the masquerade?" I bit my lower lip and waited for him to say something, anything, to let me know where I stood. "I have questions."

His fingers tapped an impatient rhythm on the desk. I forced my face to mirror his neutral expression. Finally, he stood and walked around the desk until we were inches apart. He lifted a hand, like he wanted to touch me, then let it drop to his side. "Not now. I have work to do, Ms. Donahue, and so do you." The tone of his voice softened to an intimate purr. "Call Jose. Tell him I'll be leaving for the office in thirty minutes."

"Sure. Right away." On the outside, I appeared calm, but inside, my head and heart waged war against each other. Why couldn't the man just say what he meant instead of skirting around the issue?

For the next thirty minutes, I paced the hallway. I could deal with his anger or censure, but not knowing his feelings sent my blood pressure into the ozone. The fact that he'd ignored my request to clear the air between us only exacerbated my irritation. We needed to talk, because I couldn't continue to work like this.

CHAPTER 25

ROURKE

*B*y the time Jose arrived with the car, my anxiety had transformed into anger. I went down to the lobby and out into the warm summer sunshine. Heat shimmered above the pavement. Car horns beeped, and traffic rumbled. Jose met me at the curb with a tip of his hat.

"Good morning," I said, doing my best to hide my feelings. "Mr. Menshikov will be down in a minute."

"Good morning, Ms. Donahue."

I slid into the quiet oasis of the car, and he shut the door behind me.

Five minutes later, Roman appeared. A young woman with a puppy nearly tripped over her feet when he strode out of the building. Dark sunglasses obscured his eyes. He ignored her and eased into the car across from me. He was talking into his Bluetooth, speaking rapid-fire French to a business associate, too fast for me to translate. I stared out the window while we pulled into the street. The heat of his stare burned into me from behind those expensive shades. Both hands rested on the tops of his spread thighs.

At the second stoplight, he ended his call and shifted his attention to me. "Tell me about your aunt."

The request caught me off guard. Aside from his bizarre visit to my apartment last night, he'd never inquired about my personal life. I rubbed sweaty palms over the skirt of my dress. "I've got her in a nursing home, but their care is questionable. They let her wander off, and I'm afraid she's going to get hurt or worse. I try to check on her as often as I can. It's difficult with my work schedule." I waved my hands, helplessness washing over me. "And she's on the other side of the city, so it's not like I can go there every day."

The tilt of his head signified genuine interest. "What's wrong with her?"

"She has early onset Alzheimer's and requires constant supervision. The other day, she wandered down the street. I only found out because one of the patients let it slip." Tears burned the backs of my eyelids for the loss of her freedom and the beautiful woman I'd once known. I blinked them into submission. "If anything happens to her, I'll never forgive myself."

"You love her very much," he said softly.

"Yes, I do. She took me in when my parents died, even though her husband was terminally ill with cancer. I don't know what I'd have done without her. She's the only family I have left, and I owe her so much."

When I'd had nowhere to go and no one to turn to, Aunt May had come to the rescue, offering hugs and smiles and a place in her home. Now, the tables had turned. With her husband gone, she needed me to take care of her, and I would sacrifice everything to see her comfortable and happy.

"Why don't you move her somewhere else?"

"The waiting list for a five-star facility is over a year. Full-time care is crazy expensive. Uncle Tim's illness put them into bankruptcy. The money she had left from his life insurance went to pay their bills. I can't afford anything better." Hopelessness renewed the tears. I swallowed them down, determined to stay positive. "But I have this job now, and in a few months, I may be able to get her into another place."

"I can only imagine how it must feel to see someone you love suffering." His eyes softened, warm and blue, like the Mediterranean Sea. "When my parents died, I was very young, just a baby. My adoptive father is the only parent I remember. If anything happened to that man, I'd be devastated. I'd move heaven and earth to help him. People like us, we know the value of family, especially in the wake of losing our own." The light shifted as we turned onto a different street, illuminating his chiseled brow and cheekbones, and coloring my perception of him. In the cozy space of the car, he seemed more approachable, almost human. "She's lucky to have you."

"And I'm lucky to have her," I said, thinking of all the times she'd fed me chicken soup when I'd been sick and had mended my clothes, never complaining.

"Your father was a wealthy man. He didn't leave you any money from his estate?"

I smiled at the memory of my good-natured father and his lavish spending habits. "Money was never his strong suit. He was wealthy on paper, but his debts far exceeded his assets. The people he'd trusted to invest his money had done a poor job." When the executor had closed the estate, there had been nothing left for me. "I had to sell everything to afford college tuition." Even then, the money had run out quickly, forcing me to seek employment. Everly had come to my rescue, offering a job as her assistant.

"With your determination, I'm sure you'll work something out."

I opened my mouth to reply, but his phone rang. He lifted

a finger, signaling for me to wait, and answered the call in Russian.

The interlude gave me a chance to study him. While he spoke and stared out the window, I drank in every detail of his appearance—a shadow of stubble darkened his smooth cheeks, even though he'd shaved less than a few hours ago. A tiny scar marred the tanned skin above his lip, giving his mouth an air of dangerous vulnerability. His rich voice rumbled into my ears, smooth with rough edges, fortified steel encased in velvet. The list of contradictions went on and on, too many to process and adding to my confusion.

"I apologize for the interruption," he said to me, shutting off his phone and placing it in his shirt pocket. "You were telling me about your aunt. Please continue."

"I'm worried about her. She depends on me, and I'm afraid I'll let her down."

"The girl I know will do everything in her power to get her way. You can do this, Rourke." His soft words of encouragement settled around me like a blanket.

"It's not always under my control. Not everyone has access to the same resources as you." I turned my gaze back to the window and fought the bitter taste in my mouth. "Money talks, and I don't have much."

"Money isn't always the answer."

We rode in silence for a few blocks. I had no idea how to reconcile this man with the one who'd yelled at me for putting yellow mustard on his sandwich. His unnerving stare swept over me, centering on my face until heat scalded my cheeks. A million questions flitted through my head, begging to be answered, but I bit my lower lip and held them in. The uncertainty of where we stood—where *I* stood—festered until I couldn't breathe.

"Is there something you want to say, Ms. Donahue?" Amusement curled one corner of his lips.

"I need to know where we stand," I said, fidgeting in the seat, unable to contain my burning curiosity one more second. "What happened last night? What does this mean?"

"Excuse us, Jose." With a press of a button, he raised the partition. Since my employment, I'd grown accustomed to the constant company of drivers, security, and servants. They melted into the background of my life like the white rolling clouds and clear-blue sky outside the car. "Talk."

With deliberate slowness, I donned my sunglasses to hide my thoughts from his shrewd gaze.

He touched my elbow, the warmth of his fingertips sizzling on my bare skin. "Don't hide your eyes from me." Strange words coming from a man who hid everything from everyone.

I lowered my hand anyway and met his gaze. "Aren't you a little freaked out about our situation?"

"No."

"We kissed last night, and this morning you're acting like nothing happened."

"Because nothing did happen."

"Maybe it was nothing to you, but I don't go around kissing my employers."

"We've done a lot more than kiss." His jaw tensed, becoming more square and prominent. "Or have *you* forgotten? Because I haven't. I remember every bit of how it felt to be inside you, your taste, your smell. I remember it very well." He passed a hand through his hair, mussing the perfect strands into spikes. The artful disarray contrasted with the controlled lines of his suit.

I dragged the tip of my tongue across the dry expanse of my lower lip. He remembered everything. Hearing his words brought back memories of that night —the dew on the grass, the smell of smoke and his cologne, the black velvet Surrey sky strewn with stars. "I haven't forgotten. But what happened, it changes everything."

"Why didn't you tell me who you were?" A touch of anger simmered beneath his cool tone.

"Why would I talk about it? You made it very clear that confidentiality was of the utmost importance. And, in my defense, a visit to The Devil's Playground is hardly subject matter for a job resume." His nostrils flared with an elaborate exhale. "You could have said something instead of letting me sweat all this time."

"As I recall, you're the one who walked—excuse me—*ran* away from me that night. You made me promise not to follow you or look for you. You insisted that we couldn't continue with the relationship. Your words. Not mine."

"There was no point. I was returning to New York. You're a billionaire, and I'm a working-class girl. In case you haven't noticed, our lives are worlds apart. And I didn't know I'd be working for you. If I had, I'd never—" I lifted a hand, intending to plead my case. He caught my wrist, encircling my fragile bones with his thumb and forefinger.

"Never what?" My focus fell to his lips, while my ears rejoiced over the deadly seduction in his voice. "Come to work for me? Have sex with me in a secret room of a medieval castle?" I nodded, unable to speak or look away from his haunting eyes. "But you did, my beautiful Cinderella, and I think you liked it."

"Yes," I whispered, aware of how the confession blurred the lines between propriety and desire.

"And now we deal with the consequences. There are decisions to be made."

"Which are?" The pad of his thumb swept over the back of my hand. The caress traveled all the way to my core.

"We have three choices. Do we continue what we started that night, do we put it behind us and continue like nothing happened, or do we go our separate ways?" The intensity of his stare sent a ripple of excitement through my body. His index finger tapped my wrist. "I'll leave the decision up to you."

My heart beat wildly in my chest. Continue? He wanted more? In my wildest dreams, I never thought continuing would be an option. At best, I thought we might resume our work relationship under strained circumstances. I never dreamed he'd want to see more of me in a personal capacity. "When you say 'continue,' do you mean just the sex part or something more?"

His thumb continued to stroke my hand. "I'm open to negotiations on all fronts."

CHAPTER 26

ROURKE

*F*our months ago, I'd had an intimate encounter with a mysterious stranger. If I'd known then the many ways it would change my life, I'd have done it again in a heartbeat. Sitting in the car with him, smelling his cologne, feeling the effects of his testosterone on my body, opened up a new world for me. His liquid-blue irises brimmed with heat and desire and fear. The sensation of power and control buoyed my confidence. This man could buy anything he wanted, yet he desired me.

"I'm not sure what I want," I said, and it was the truth. The complications of a relationship with my employer and a man of secrets carried a lot of risks for my career and my heart.

"I know I'm not an easy person to work for." I snorted at his words, and he shot me a dirty smirk. "My expectations are high. I demand a lot from my employees and even more from my friends." He rolled his lips together, drawing my gaze to their fullness and making me want to taste them again. "Any woman who's with me has to be prepared to make some concessions. But if you're willing to take a chance, I'd like very much to know you better."

The ache in my chest spread into my lungs. He seemed uncertain, almost fearful of my rejection. I stroked my fingertips along the side of his face. He closed his eyes, his breath stuttering when my touch reached the curve of his jaw. "I need to think about it."

"Take your time," he said. The pulse above his collarbone fluttered. I wanted to lay my lips on it, to taste the salt of his skin. Jose's voice floated over the intercom.

"Mr. Menshikov, sorry to interrupt. We're about five minutes away."

"Thank you." The muscles in his throat constricted as he swallowed. I drew my hand away and relaxed into the seat. A subtle shift occurred in his demeanor. The line of his jaw tensed. His shoulders straightened, chest broadened. He twitched the knot in his tie and glanced at his wristwatch. "Right on time. When we get upstairs, I want you in the conference room with me to take notes. Keep an eye on Gaylord, the CFO. He's a slimy bastard. Whenever he's stressed, his left eye twitches. And be careful what you say. None of these people can be trusted. Got it?" The vulnerability in his eyes disappeared, replaced by shrewd intellect and a predatory gleam. He grabbed the handle of his briefcase. The car stopped in front of the building. He shifted in his seat, preparing to exit, but stopped to look at me.

"Yes. Got it." I nodded, thinking he wanted affirmation.

"Brandy," he said. I bristled at the thought of the pretty girl and their night together, my fingernails digging into the leather seat. "And the condoms. I didn't fuck her."

Jose opened the door, and Roman got out, leaving me behind to process what he'd just said.

"Coming?" Roman extended a hand to help me from the

car. I took it; my fingers grazed over his palm, sending tremors of delight along my nerve endings.

The opportunity for questions escaped before I drew my next breath. He dropped my hand and strode into the lobby. We rode the elevator in silence. There were too many people to allow for private conversation. I stared at his reflection in the stainless-steel elevator doors. He stared back.

A dozen board members greeted us in the conference room. They stood when Roman entered. While he shook hands and accepted introductions, I settled our things at the table and went for coffee. When I returned, he pulled out my chair for me but didn't acknowledge my presence in any other way.

Gaylord sat to my left and dropped a hand onto my forearm. He was shorter than me, immaculately dressed in a navy suit. He smiled at me with small, yellowish teeth. "Get me a coffee, would you, honey?"

Roman had been conversing with the woman to his right. Hearing Gaylord's request, he turned to face us. Beneath the table, his hand found my thigh and squeezed, preventing me from moving. "Stay."

"I don't mind," I said.

"No. You work for me." His eyes narrowed, but his next words were for his colleague. "Get your own coffee, Gaylord."

"I just assumed," he asked, but he withdrew his hand from my arm.

"Well, don't." Roman's lethal tone brought the conference room to a standstill. "Ms. Donahue is here to assist me, not fetch your coffee. You'll treat her with respect."

The color drained from Gaylord's face. I almost laughed out loud. He swallowed and cleared his throat before glancing nervously at me. "I apologize, Ms. Donahue."

"Apology accepted," I said, giving him a tight smile.

For the rest of the day, everyone tiptoed around Roman. By reproaching Gaylord, he'd set the tone for the meeting and had established himself as the alpha. While I took notes, I studied the way he manipulated the conversations. Not only was he handsome and smart, but he understood human nature and used it to get what he wanted. Every minute we spent together peeled away another layer of his personality and added to the intrigue.

At the end of the day, he ushered me downstairs to the waiting car. With his hand on the small of my back, he said, "Jose, we're going to make a stop on the way home." He dipped his lips to my ear. The heat of his breath on my earlobe sent gooseflesh rippling down my neck. "Give him your aunt's address. I want to meet her."

❦

The nurses and orderlies stared at Roman as we walked down the dingy corridors to Aunt May's room. I rubbed my nose, trying to wipe away the stale smell of the facility. My cheeks burned with embarrassment. Although he never commented, I could tell by the tight line of his mouth and the sweep of his gaze that he found the place repugnant.

"You don't have to do this," I said for the third time, wishing he would have waited in the car.

"I know that." We stopped outside her room. He stared down at me before sweeping a lock of my hair away from my face.

I knocked on the door. Aunt May sat in a chair facing the window.

"Hi, Aunt May. How are you?"

Her blue eyes carried a blank stare, one I'd never seen before. "I'm fine. Thank you. How are you?"

"I'm good." I dropped a kiss on the top of her head. "This is my boss, Roman."

"Nice to meet you," he said. They shook hands, but I could tell something was off by the tilt of her head. "I've heard a lot of good things about you," he continued.

"You have?" For the briefest moment, her gaze brightened. Two seconds later, the spark flickered and extinguished. She studied my face. "Who are you again?"

Her question sliced into me like an icy dagger. I'd been dreading this moment since she'd received her diagnosis three years ago. Now that the time had come, I didn't want to believe it. "I'm Rourke, your niece. Martha's daughter?"

"Martha has a daughter?" Her eyebrows lifted in surprise. She shook her head and laughed. "Oh, that's priceless. Martha's too young to have a daughter. She can't be more than twenty."

I stared at her, stunned, my heart breaking in two. She was my only link to my parents, the last piece of family in my life. If she didn't remember me, then I didn't exist anymore. "No. I'm Rourke. Remember?" I clasped her hand in mine. The polite smile on her face had been reserved for strangers, and now it was meant for me—a stranger.

"She's been like that for a few days now." An orderly entered the room, pushing a tray of beige-colored food on a cart.

"Why didn't someone call me?" Tears blurred my vision.

Roman smoothed a hand over my shoulder and down my back.

"There's nothing you can do," the orderly said with a shake of her head.

"You'll have to excuse me. It's time for dinner." Aunt May

turned back to the window, uninterested in the food or me. "Thank you for stopping by. What was your name again?"

"Rourke," I said through a throat clogged by emotion.

Roman led me to the car. I held it together until the door shut behind us. Once we were inside, I fell apart. The sobs came in a rush, one after another, shaking my body. I buried my face in my hands, not wanting him to see my breakdown but unable to control it.

"Hey, hey." In an instant, he was across the car, pulling me into his arms and cradling me like a small child. His big hands smoothed my hair. Twice I felt the brush of his lips on my temple. "It's okay. Go ahead and cry. Let it all out. I've got you."

I cried from one side of the city to the other. My tears made a dark, wet circle on his jacket. The unfairness of the situation hurt my heart. Aunt May didn't deserve this, and there was nothing I could do. Even though I'd been preparing myself for this day, I had no idea how much it would hurt to sit at her side and watch the once-vibrant woman fade away.

"I'm sorry." A trail of wetness traced down my cheeks. I pulled away, embarrassed by the outburst. Somehow, I'd moved to his lap, buttressed by his hard chest and two strong arms.

"Don't apologize. I'm feeling a little misty-eyed myself." With the corner of his silk handkerchief, he dabbed at my tears then tweaked my nose. "Blow."

I did as he requested then tried to salvage the last of my mascara. "No one carries handkerchiefs anymore." My voice shook, weakened by the outpouring of feelings.

"Call me old-fashioned." The humor in his tone brought my gaze up to his. Warmth lightened his features. The pain in my chest ebbed. "Better?"

"Yes. Thank you. I—I don't usually break down like this." In fact, I never cried in front of anyone, not even Everly. The release of emotion left me raw and exhausted. Awareness of his body dawned. He was big and male and strong. In his arms, I felt safe.

"When I'm upset, I usually throw things," he said.

"I know."

"You should try it sometime." His hand rested on my knee. He squeezed. An immediate pulse of desire hit between my legs. Lord have mercy, he smelled good enough to eat. I sucked in a breath, slid from his lap onto the seat, and adjusted my clothes.

"I'll be fine," I said, trying to put some emotional distance between us.

Jose came around the car to let us out. Instead of striding ahead, leaving me at the curb, Roman kept pace at my side and waited for me to board the elevator before entering. When we reached the penthouse, he hesitated in the foyer.

"I'm going to go change clothes. Do you need anything?" I asked. Usually, after work, he went straight to his study and stayed there to tie up loose ends and prepare for the upcoming day.

"Have dinner with me." His hand found mine, large palm sliding over my small one, lighting my nerve endings on fire.

"I don't know." A hot bath and mindless television sounded like heaven. I needed time to process the events of the day. His close proximity, the headiness of his cologne, the heat of his body, had muddled my thoughts. "I'm exhausted."

"An even better reason to have dinner with me. Go put on your sweats, and when you come back, I'll have Chef whip up something simple for us. No stress. No work. Just you and me and a nice bottle of wine." He finished the request with a kiss to the back of my hand.

If I went back to my apartment, I'd spend the night alone, crying and feeling sorry for myself. No girl in her right mind would turn down dinner with Prince Charming. The feeling of his lips against my skin, warm and soft, and the hopefulness in his eyes broke my resolve. "Alright."

CHAPTER 27

ROURKE

Thirty minutes later, I walked into Roman's living room. Soft piano music hung in the air, and the aromas of garlic and oregano wafted in from the kitchen. Through the wall of windows, a starless black sky blanketed the city. It was the first time I'd been there as a guest and not an employee. The shift in status presented the apartment from a new perspective. A nervous flutter in my belly prompted me to stop beside the suede sofa and take a deep breath.

What was I doing? I'd never taken risks, not because I didn't want to, but because I'd never been given the opportunity. The moment Roman had walked into my life, all that had changed, and I liked it. Despite my anxieties, I wanted to see where fate might lead me, and I was willing to accept the consequences.

Ivan met me at the base of the staircase. His black gaze traveled over my T-shirt and yoga pants. I ran a self-conscious hand through my hair, aware of how this looked.

"Good evening, Ms. Donahue," he said, a smug smirk on his lips.

"Good evening." Something about his expression made me blush, even though I had every right to be here. For all he knew, I was assisting Roman in some capacity. He continued through the room, and I followed on his heels.

Roman came down the steps a few seconds later. "Hey," he said in his rich voice. A white T-shirt hugged the muscles of his torso. Soft gray sweatpants hung low on his hips. The casual clothes and day's growth of beard gave him a youthful air.

"Hi." Static electricity crackled between us. Once again, we were standing on the edge of uncharted territory. He extended a hand. I hesitated. If I accepted, we'd be breaching the fragile boundaries of our work relationship. Then again, we'd already broken all the rules. "Um, what about them?" My fingers slid between his at the same moment the kitchen staff bustled into the dining room, trays of aromatic food in their hands. They nodded in greeting, their gazes sweeping over our clasped hands, rife with judgment.

"It's okay." With a proprietary tug, he pulled me into his side. The heat of his body seeped through the thin fabric of our clothes, awakening all the cells and synapses in my body. "It's not their place to question my actions."

At the quizzical lift of his brows, I rolled my lips together and tried to explain. "You're the employer. You don't have to worry about what your employees say. But they *will* talk among themselves, and it could undermine my working relationship with them if they think I'm screwing the boss."

"I see." He nodded but didn't release my hand, pulling me instead toward the dining room.

"No, you don't see." I balked.

"I'll take care of it. You worry too much." With another tug, he escorted me toward the food.

The dining room was situated on the corner of the apartment, at the intersection of two perpendicular glass walls, providing a one-hundred eighty-degree view of New York City. Dozens of tiny candles illuminated the space, their flames reflecting off the windows and bathing everything in golden light.

"This is lovely," I said. My hands began to tremble. I was really doing this. Once I crossed the threshold from employee to date, there would be no going back. Did I really want to risk my future and my aunt's for a fling? His fingers closed tighter around mine.

"Relax. It's just dinner," he said.

"Right." A brittle smile stretched my face. No matter how badly I wanted to believe him, the risks remained real. If anything went wrong, he'd continue with his perfect life, and I'd be left with ruined professional and personal reputations.

"Rourke, look at me." Using his thumb and forefinger to capture my chin, he tilted my face up. His eyes were soft, blue, and sincere. "Nothing will happen between us unless you want it to. You're in complete control."

The soothing tone of his voice eased my anxieties. When I nodded, he dipped his lips to mine in a chaste kiss. He tasted of mint, his mouth relaxed and pliable. As I breathed in his spicy cologne, a sense of calm washed over me. Although the odds were against us, if this relationship worked, it would be worth the risk. *He* was worth the risk.

"Kate. Michael." At his call, the maid and chef appeared in the doorway. "You're dismissed for the night. Thank you. Have a good evening."

They melted into the shadows of the apartment, leaving us to dine in solitude. Roman made casual conversation, asking questions about my childhood and my relationship with Everly. After a while, it was easy to forget that he was one of the wealthiest men in the world. Without his power suit and briefcase, he seemed like a regular guy.

After the second glass of wine, my inhibitions began to

relax. "I've told you all about myself, but I don't know anything about you."

"I doubt that," he said, eyes sparkling.

"Okay, I may have done a few Google searches on you." A blush burned my cheeks. "But Wikipedia doesn't have much to say beyond the basics."

He shrugged, pausing to top off my wineglass before continuing. "What do you want to know?"

"Tell me about your childhood." A shadow passed across his face. I bit my lower lip, wishing I could take back the request. "You don't have to."

"No. It's okay." After a sip of wine, he swirled the liquid around the glass and stared at the contents. "My parents fled their country in the middle of the night, in the midst of a revolution. Ivan coordinated the escape. We split up. I went with Ivan, while my parents took a different route. My parents never made it. At the border, insurgents beheaded them both. Ivan smuggled me into the United States and placed me with Nicky's family. I grew up under an alias, my identity kept secret, until the regime fell from power and the threat of danger had dissipated."

My heart ached for his loss. I placed my hand over his and squeezed. "Is that why you can't go after Milada?"

He nodded. "There are still people over there who would love to have my head. Claudette knows that."

"But you had a happy childhood?"

"I did. In fact, I had no idea I was born a prince until I turned fourteen. My adoptive parents wanted me to grow up as normal as possible. They gave me unconditional love and all the opportunities I could ever ask for." His palm slid over mine, our fingers entwining. "Aside from the untimely deaths of my parents, I have no regrets." He shifted in his chair before bringing my knuckles to his lips. "I haven't spoken to anyone about it in years. It's in the past." Another kiss to my hand made my nipples tighten. God, he was glorious like this, unguarded, relaxed, and attentive. His eyes met mine, and I clenched my thighs together to stave off the ache of desire. "I'm more interested in the future—in us."

❦

*T*hree weeks later, I had to fight back a goofy grin as I waited for Roman in his study. We'd spent the days working together. On the evenings where he didn't have business obligations, we watched movies in his theater room, holding hands and making out like teenagers. The evenings had left me wanting more—more kisses, more handholding, more Roman.

"Good morning, Ms. Donahue," he said, approaching with Ivan on his heels.

"Good morning, Mr. Menshikov," I replied. Our eyes met, and his face lit up with a genuine smile. The unexpected pleasure of it hit me low in the gut. I smiled back, aware of Ivan's speculative gaze bouncing between us.

Roman paused to run the back of a finger along the slope of my cheek. "I'll be flying to Edinburgh on Thursday. Make the arrangements, would you?"

"Already done," I replied.

"And see if my table at Swerve is available for tonight. I'm meeting Gaylord for dinner."

"Sure. Anything else?"

"Yes. One more thing." His eyes searched mine, sending a blast of heat and longing straight to the apex of my thighs. "If you could get your aunt into any facility, where would it be?"

"Whispering Willows," I said without hesitation. The full-care nursing home was by far the best in the state, but the annual cost exceeded my yearly salary by a few thousand. The probability of getting her admitted exceeded my wildest dreams.

Roman turned to Ivan. "Make that happen, would you?" He released my chin and they continued into the study, closing the door behind them. I stood in the hallway, staring after them, and blinked back tears of disbelief.

After a few seconds, I regained my composure. As much as I appreciated his efforts, I'd never be able to afford the fees of a topnotch facility like Whispering Willows. With shaking hands, I tapped out a quick text to him.

Me: I appreciate the offer, but I'll never be able to afford it.

An answer came immediately.

Him: Maybe you can't, but I can.

Me: I can't accept. It's too much.

I held my breath and waited for his reply, but it never came. A half hour later, we met at the elevator in preparation for the drive to his office. "The nursing home—it's very generous of you, but there's no way I can accept."

"Bullshit." He glanced at his watch and pressed the elevator button for a second time. "You can and you will."

"I'm serious." We both faced the elevator doors. My back-side prickled with awareness of Ivan's presence behind us, certain the old fox was absorbing every word of our conversation.

"So am I."

The three of us boarded the car and began the long descent to the lobby. Ivan stood in front of us, closest to the doors, his hands clasped in front of him. Roman's shoulder grazed my bare arm. His little finger slipped around mine. The small gesture cracked my composure. I turned and stared up at the straight line of his nose, the sharp angles of his jaw and cheekbones, the proud tilt of his chin. He looked every bit the proud, enigmatic, exiled prince—*my* prince.

"You're impossible," I said.

"I know." He avoided my gaze, but the corners of his eyes crinkled in amusement. "I'm surprised it's taken you this long to figure it out."

CHAPTER 28

ROURKE

*A*fter lunch, Roman left for his meeting with Gaylord, and I went back to the penthouse to prepare for his trip. There were tons of small details to be completed. His wardrobe needed coordinated. Appointments and meetings had to be rearranged. Reservations had to be scheduled. I spent the afternoon in a flurry of activity.

At the end of the day, I went upstairs. Inside his bedroom, I paused to reflect on the space from a different perspective. We hadn't had sex yet, but the moment was imminent. Would he bring me here, to his massive king-size bed with its pristine white sheets and luxurious throws? Or would he take me somewhere special? I bit my lower lip, basking in the excitement of a new relationship.

If I'd learned anything from my time with Roman, it was this: speculation about his behavior was futile. I treasured his unpredictability and the thrill of never knowing where he might lead me.

I pushed aside my romantic daydreams and buckled down to the task of pulling together his wardrobe. Inside the massive walk-in closet, I paused to do a search on the weather in Edinburgh during the month of September. During my investigation, my work phone buzzed with an incoming call. A glance at the caller ID revealed Nicky's name.

He'd been conspicuously absent since our dinner, but I'd been too engrossed in Roman to notice. Now, the sight of his adopted brother's name sucked all the moisture from my mouth. For a brief moment, I considered letting the call go to voicemail then reconsidered. It was better to deal with Nicky right away. In my panic, I dropped a set of jewel-encrusted cufflinks. On my hands and knees, I searched for the missing items while cradling the phone against my ear.

"Hello?" I groped beneath the center island for the cufflinks. They were Roman's favorite pair. If I'd lost them, he'd be livid.

"Hello, princess," he said. "I'm downstairs. Can I come up?"

"Roman's out," I said, deciding to keep our conversation short and direct.

"I know. It's you I've come to see."

My fingertips nudged something, but it rolled out of reach. After another moment of groping, I wrapped my fingers around something long and cylindrical. "I don't think that's a good idea."

"Come on. It's important or I wouldn't bother you. It'll only take a minute."

"Alright. I have a few things I want to talk to you about, too." This might not be the ideal opportunity, but I wanted to let him know exactly where he could shove his extortion attempt. Then I looked down at the item in my hand. A tube of lipstick.

A dozen thoughts ran through my head at once. Why would Roman have lipstick in his bedroom unless a woman had been in here? Aside from the housekeeper, no one came in here but the two of us. The lipstick hadn't been there when I'd reorganized the closet, which meant it had somehow made its way up here since then. I closed my fingers around the tube and closed my eyes. Jealousy quickly gave way to pain. Although I'd assumed he wasn't seeing anyone else, we hadn't had that discussion yet. Did I have a right to be upset when we weren't exclusive?

I shoved the tube into my pocket and hurried downstairs. At the mirror in the hallway, I paused long enough to check my reflection. Hurt blue eyes stared back at me. After a deep breath, I schooled my features into indifference. When Roman came back, I'd ask him for the truth. Until then, I didn't want to give Nicky additional fodder for blackmail.

The elevator doors opened just as I stepped into the foyer. He greeted me with a wide smile and a peck on each cheek. I didn't smile back at him. "I'm not in the mood for your games. What do you need?"

"Wow. You sound just like Roman." He pretended to pout before brushing past me and into the living room.

"Whatever you have to say, say it," I said, fingering the lipstick in my pocket.

"I thought you might want some company tonight, since Roman's busy." His comment sent a shiver of foreboding up my spine.

"No, thank you. I've got work to do."

"Really?" Dark eyebrows lifted. He turned, a wide smile on his lips, eyes twinkling with mischief. "I assumed you'd be free. I just bumped into Roman at The Devil's Playground. He'll probably be there all night, knowing him."

I didn't hear the rest of what he said; his words obscured by the buzzing in my ears. "I thought he was having dinner at Swerve." I turned my attention to a nonexistent piece of lint on my sweater in an effort to hide the hurt. Betrayal stung like a motherfucker. Its cruel, careless claws sliced through my heart. In an effort to assuage the pain, I pressed a hand to my chest.

"Are you okay?" Nicky rushed to my side. Taking my elbow, he led me to the sofa.

"Fine. Heartburn," I said, unable to form a complete sentence. My ribs expanded, creaking with the effort to breathe through the ache.

"Can I get you some water?" His shrewd gaze searched my face. I shook my head and smiled, unwilling to let him see the way he'd breached my armor. He smiled back. "Okay. Good." He took my hand in his. "So, tell me about you. What's been going on?"

I withdrew my hand and wiped it across my thigh. "If you came here to coerce me into playing more games, you're wasting my time. Roman knows everything."

The dying daylight from the windows caught the auburn highlights in his hair as he cocked his head to one side. "You came clean? Nice move. I didn't give you nearly enough credit." He tapped a finger to his chin. "That changes things considerably. I'm going to have to reassess my—" He halted midsentence. "Wait. Oh, no. You've fallen for him, haven't you?"

"Get out." I stood, suddenly too weary to continue pretending my feelings didn't exist.

"I'm so sorry. Here you are, waiting in his penthouse, doing his work, while he's out fucking everything that moves." The smile fell from his face, and his voice lowered to a sympathetic croon. "Poor Cinderella. I tried to save you." He chucked me under the chin. "Well, don't berate yourself too much. You're not the first, and you certainly won't be the last."

🌸

*B*ack in my apartment, I stared at my bedroom ceiling until dawn illuminated the room in shades of pink and lavender. In my head, I scrolled through all the evenings Roman had been absent from the penthouse. How many of those nights had been spent watching or participating in the hedonistic pleasures of The Devil's Playground? Bitter tears burned my eyes, but I fought them back. I refused to cry over a man who'd betrayed my trust. Even though we hadn't discussed the terms of our relationship, I'd assumed we were headed toward some type of commitment. Boy, was I a fool. Of course he had other women. He was Roman Menshikov. Men like him didn't believe in monogamy. He was an exiled prince, a man of lusty appetites, and a billionaire. By his own admission, he could have anything or anyone he wanted. More tears blurred my vision.

When my alarm went off, I threw it across the room and went back to bed. An hour later, someone knocked on my door. Wearing nothing but a T-shirt and panties, I stalked to the door. "What?"

"Are you okay?" Roman's voice floated through the door. "It's six-thirty."

Shit. I'd expected Julie or Ivan or one of the other servants. Not Satan himself. "No. I'm not feeling well." I'd never been late since my employment.

"Let me in."

"No. I'll be fine. I just need to rest." My insides quaked. I leaned my back against the door and waited for his reply.

"Can I get you anything?"

His concern resurrected my anger. Too little, too late. "No. I'm going back to bed. I'm sure I'll be fine tomorrow." I needed time to process what had happened and consider my options. In the meantime, I couldn't face him or more of his deceptions.

Once he left, I dressed and headed down to the street. The idea of spending more time in his high tower, locked away, made my stomach turn. Each piece of furniture, every priceless painting and sculpture, bore his stamp. Outside, I walked in the chilly fall air until my feet hurt and my legs ached. Then, I boarded the subway and went to visit Aunt May. I needed to be around someone who loved me, even if she didn't remember who I was anymore.

❀

When I reached the nursing home, I sat with Aunt May in the facility rec room. She didn't recognize me, but her presence offered comfort. I poured out the entire story to her, from the beginning, leaving out the sexy parts. She listened intently, and somewhere in the middle of my ramblings, the shadow passed from her eyes.

"You love him, don't you?" she asked, patting my knee.

I'd been cradling my head in my hands but looked up at her touch. "Auntie?"

"Oh, sweetie. You've gone and fallen for this man." The clear blue of her eyes exactly matched the hue of mine and my mother's.

"I've missed you so much." In a flash, I threw my arms around here, squeezing her frail bones until she grunted.

"I've missed you, too." Her fragile hands soothed up and down my back. "Now, sit down, and let's talk through this."

It felt good to have her back with me, even if it was only for a few precious moments. "I think I made a mistake."

"Have you asked him to explain?"

"No. Not yet." Confrontation had never been my strong suit. What if he said Nicky's accusations were true?

"Well, you can't jump to conclusions. This Nicky person isn't a trustworthy source. You said yourself that he'll twist things around to suit his needs." Her smile filled me with warmth.

"Excuse me, Ms. Donahue. May I speak with you a moment?" The facility director mustered a polite smile.

"Sure." I cupped Aunt May's cheek. "I'll be right back."

"I didn't mean to interrupt, but I wanted to let you know that the transfer to Whispering Willows has come through." The furrow between his bushy eyebrows signified his displeasure.

"Already?" In the confusion of the day, I'd forgotten Roman's order to Ivan. The waiting list for admission exceeded a year. Surely he hadn't been able to get her in within the day. Then again, he was Roman Menshikov and he always got what he wanted.

"Yes. They called today to make arrangements. She'll be moving within the week."

Given the circumstances of the previous night, I had no idea how to pay the fees at such an expensive place, but I wasn't going to punish Aunt May for my mistakes. I'd find a way to get the money if I had to sell myself to do it.

"Thanks," I said. "Does Aunt May know?"

"Not yet. I thought you'd want to tell her yourself." He nodded and shook my hand. "Good afternoon, Ms. Donahue."

"Good afternoon." I made my way back to Aunt May, eager to break the good news. The moment our eyes met, disappointment extinguished my excitement.

"Hello," she said. Lines of worry bracketed her mouth. "Do I know you?"

CHAPTER 29

ROURKE

*A*fter a disappointing day, I called up Mena and Christian for moral support. We had dinner and a few drinks. I told them a little bit about the conflicts between me, my employer, and his adoptive brother. I couldn't bring myself to talk about my feelings for Roman. Even though I was angry with him, speaking of our personal relationship felt like a betrayal to both of us.

As we left the bar, Christian stopped me on the sidewalk. "You look amazing. Whatever you're doing, keep it up."

"What? A compliment from Christian?" Mena rolled her eyes dramatically. "It's rarer than a unicorn sighting. Consider yourself lucky." She stroked a hand down the arm of my pinstriped blouse. "Don't listen to me. I'm just jealous. He's right. You look fantastic."

"Thanks." To relieve my frustrations, I'd spent a lot of time in Roman's gym and running. Their praise bolstered my confidence.

"You're welcome to stay with me tonight," Mena said. "Maybe some time away from this guy will give you a new perspective.

As tempting as her invitation was, cowardice had never been a profitable endeavor for me. "I appreciate the offer, but I should go home."

"Suit yourself." We hugged and promised to get together more often before going our separate ways.

I flagged down a taxi and shivered in the back seat. Fall loomed around the corner. The nights grew chillier, while the days offered bright sunshine. Everly would be home soon, and I couldn't wait to see her. Despite Mena and Christian's company, the events of the day had left a feeling of emptiness. Times like these made me miss my parents.

I picked up my phone and switched it on. A dozen text messages and voicemails flooded the display screen.

Roman: *How are you feeling?*

Roman: *Call me.*

Roman: *Did you go to the doctor?*

Roman: *Can I bring you anything?*

Roman: *Where are you?*

Guilt turned to acid in my stomach. Despite his packed schedule today, he'd been worried about me. I dropped my phone back into my purse. With my lower lip drawn between my teeth, I watched the bright city lights flicker past. I wanted to believe he cared. Had he gone to The Devil's Playground because I wasn't able to satisfy his needs? During my travels with Everly, I'd been around authoritative men. Rumors of infidelity and sexual appetites always drifted in their wakes. In my experience, Roman was more male, more alpha, than all of them combined. Maybe I wasn't enough for a man who could have anyone or anything he wanted with a snap of his fingers. Maybe he sought the thrill of the chase, and now that he had me in his sights, he'd lost interest.

The hands of the lobby clock pointed toward midnight when I finally entered Roman's building and boarded the elevator. I stared at the numbers above the door. My pulse escalated with every passing floor. When I stepped out of the car and into the foyer, I had to rest a hand on the wall to steady myself. Roman often worked into the early hours of the morning. With a little luck, I might be able to sneak to my room unnoticed.

The blue light of the full moon bathed Roman's living room. I slipped off my shoes and padded barefoot down the hall toward my apartment. The bright, silvery orb passed behind a bank of clouds, shifting the room into darkness. I unlocked the door and went inside, not bothering to flip on the lights. Halfway to my bedroom, the hair stood on the back of my neck. A shadowy figure sat on the wingback chair in the corner, in the shape of a man. I yelped and dropped my shoes. They landed on the floor with a clunk. Roman switched on the lamp next to him. A shiver ran down my back. Hurt and anger and jealousy swelled to a crescendo between us. The room crackled with the intensity of emotions.

"You shouldn't be in here," I said crossly. "It's a violation of privacy."

"I thought you were sick." The moon reappeared, casting the angles and planes of his face in sharp relief. Danger and strength sizzled in the powerful lines of his body. My head swam, intoxicated by his anger. I placed a hand on the back of the sofa to bolster my quaking knees.

"I was sick, and now I'm not." What was it about him that kept me so enthralled? His arrogance and unpredictability drew me in with a gravitational force too strong to resist. He was the hunter, I was the prey, and I reveled in the hunt.

"Where have you been?" he asked.

A bitter snort escaped before I could stop it. "I should be asking you that. Where have *you* been?"

"I've been working all day. You know where I was." The amount of hurt in his voice sent me back a pace. Then I saw the melted candles, the bouquet of flowers, and the cold food on the dining room table. "I was worried."

"Right." A pang of guilt twisted my insides, but I pushed it away. I didn't owe him anything. Not after what he'd done. Even though we hadn't set boundaries for our relationship, I still felt betrayed.

"Why are you acting like this?" The line of his shoulders bowed, as if weighted by a burden too heavy to bear. Another wave of guilt flowed through me.

"I know where you were last night. You were at The Devil's Playground." The accusation burst out of me before I could stop it.

His fingers curled into the armrest of the chair, but his face remained implacable. "Who told you that?"

"Nicky."

"Of course. That bastard can't stand to see me happy." A shuddering breath shook his shoulders. "This is why I told you to stay away from him. He's toxic."

At his admission, my insides collapsed. The truth hurt more than I'd anticipated. He'd been with someone else. Maybe multiple others. I wanted to fall to my knees and wail, but I wouldn't give him the satisfaction of seeing how badly I was hurt. Unable to bear the pain, I shifted the emotion into anger and shook a finger in his face. "You lied to me. How could you do that? I trusted you."

He grabbed my finger, wrapping his hand around it, pulling me toward him, the pressure gentle but commanding. "Yes, I was there. With Gaylord. He's joining the club." I wanted to believe him, more than anything, but I couldn't trust him. Not yet. "It was business, Rourke. Nothing else."

"Did you—did you participate or just watch?" Jealousy erased my common sense. The thought of him near any other woman liquefied my brain. I wanted to hurt him and anyone else who'd touched his proud body. "Is that why we haven't slept with each other? Are you getting it somewhere else?" A sob caught in my throat.

His face contorted, lines of pain deepening around his eyes and mouth at the sound of my distress. "Goddammit." His nostrils flared. Icy blue eyes narrowed. "We haven't slept with each other because I wanted to take it slow and get to know you without the confusion that comes with sex. We're walking on a slippery slope here, Rourke. You're my employee. I'm in a sticky situation."

So, this was how it felt to be in love. Waves of pain and longing and need more intense than anything I'd ever known undulated through me. On the outside, I willed myself to remain calm, impassive, but inside, I screamed at the injustice of it.

"Is that what you're worried about? Are you afraid I'll sue you for sexual harassment?" I grasped for a way to hurt him the way he'd hurt me. "Do you need me to sign a waiver like one of your 'girlfriends'?" With my free hand, I drew air quotes around the term with my fingers. "Don't worry. I'm not going to take any of your precious money." Too late, I recognized the flash of his temper in the darkness of his gaze.

"I don't give a fuck about the money." With a deft twist of his arm, he maneuvered my arm behind my back. "Enough of this bullshit." The movement brought my breasts flat against his chest. His grip buried in my hair, tilting my face up to his. "I like it when you're jealous."

"I'm not jealous." Every heaving breath rubbed my nipples against his hard torso until they were painfully erect.

"Yes, you are." His dark eyes glittered dangerously. This was the man I'd met at Bellingham Manor, the one who'd seduced and pleasured me within an inch of my life. "Put your claws in, kitten. I haven't cheated on you. In fact, I haven't been with anyone but you since we met."

I tried to wriggle free, but he held me tighter. The buttons of his dress shirt cut into my sternum. "Why should I believe you?"

"Because I love you, Rourke." His tone softened, and the grip on the back of my head gentled. "And I'm trying really hard not to fuck this up."

The weight of his declaration settled over me. I drew in a deep breath. He smelled so good, his unique blend of cologne and soap hitting my senses, making me drunk. With all my heart, I wanted to believe him. "I found a lipstick underneath the island in your closet. Can you explain that?"

The muscle beneath his cheekbone twitched. Our lips hovered millimeters apart. His breath tickled my mouth. "I'm pretty sure, if you look closely, you'll see that it's yours. When you dropped your clutch at the masquerade, it fell out, and you left it behind."

"You kept it all this time?" He nodded. Tears burned the backs of my eyelids. Why would he do that? The answer made the walls of my throat constrict.

"Don't cry, baby," he whispered.

"I'm sorry." The apology seemed inadequate to express my remorse. He released my wrist. I wrapped my arms around his neck and pulled him closer. We stood in the moonlight for a long time, holding each other, not speaking.

"The next time you have questions, I want you to come to me right away. Understand?" His voice was rough around the edges, thick and brittle with emotion.

"Yes." I buried my face deeper into the curve of his neck. "But you need to tell me what's going on with you. I don't like being the last to know."

"I promise." He threaded his fingers through mine and pulled me toward the bedroom. "Come on."

My heartrate tripled with each step closer to the bed. When we reached the mattress, he bent his head and kissed me. The softness of his lips made my blood sing. I curled my fingers into his shoulders. Our tongues tangled in a leisurely dance.

"I'm going to worship you," he said. Despite the darkness, his eyes shone with heat. "Tomorrow, we'll figure all this out. But tonight, let me show you how much I love you."

The only noise in the room was the sound of our heavy breathing. His fingers unfastened the buttons of my blouse. I shrugged out of it, letting it fall to the floor in a whisper of fabric. The gentle glide of his hands over my breasts and down my belly brought ripples of gooseflesh. He kneeled on the floor in front of me and placed his cheek against my belly. I held him to me, giving him comfort and taking his strength. The scratch of his five o'clock shadow on my bare skin did crazy things to my insides. I'd never needed anyone like this before, like I couldn't breathe without him. He'd become the oxygen that fueled my heart and lungs. Him. Only him.

"You have no idea how long I've wanted you like this." His breath tickled on my skin as he feathered butterfly kisses down to my pubic bone. "You and me. Alone. No one watching. Just us." Large hands pulled my panties over my hips and smoothed along my legs, guiding the silk to the floor.

The sight of this formidable man on his knees in front of me broke down the last of my resistance. I moaned at the touch of his tongue to my sex and dug my fingers into his hair. The combination of warmth and wetness on my delicate flesh reduced me to a wanton mess. He hooked one of my legs over his broad shoulder, opening me to him, lapping along my folds with the flat side of his tongue. When my legs began to shake, he eased me onto the edge of the bed.

"Our first time should have been like this," he said. "In a bed, just the two of us."

From above me, he unbuttoned his shirt and tossed it

aside then stepped out of his trousers. The sight of his long, tanned legs, dusted with black hair, and the bulge beneath his boxer briefs renewed my trembling.

"I don't regret any of it." I drew my hands down his sides, enjoying the texture of his skin against my palms.

"I'm a selfish bastard. No one's ever going to see your body naked again. No one but me. I want this all to myself." He cupped my sex. "Are we clear?"

"Yes." I scooted backward on the bed. He followed me, walking up the mattress on his hands and knees between my legs. The act was so primal, so animalistic, that I whimpered in anticipation of what he was going to do to me.

"Are you on birth control?" The weight of his hips pressed against mine. Something hard and thick pressed against the inside of my thigh. Jesus, I'd forgotten how big he was. My inner muscles clenched in preparation for the burn of intrusion.

"I get a shot every twelve weeks." My voice sounded husky and foreign. I ran my tongue over the dry expanse of my lips. His thighs spread mine wider.

"Good," he said and shoved into me.

The unexpected friction tore a moan of ecstasy from my throat. When the full weight of his body lowered onto mine, I reveled in the sensation of being conquered. Heat emanated from his body, like holding a live coal between my legs. He continued to press into me, going deeper, until the tip of his cock touched my deepest place. I squirmed, trying to get away, fighting to bring him closer, unable to deal with too many sensations at once.

"Oh, God," I murmured and squeezed my eyes shut. The muscles of his buttocks flexed beneath my grasping hands.

"Look at me, Rourke. Look at us." He directed my gaze down to where we were joined. I watched him slide in and out of me with long, leisurely strokes. "This is me loving you."

Every push and pull of his hips sent delicious pleasure through my body. We fell into a slow, rocking rhythm. Our bodies worked together, instinctively knowing when to pause or move, how to maximize the pleasure. All the while, Roman dropped kisses along my forehead, cheeks, neck, and breasts.

Afterward, he nestled me into the crook of his shoulder. One of his arms wrapped around my waist, holding me close. Contentment washed over me. Exhaustion followed swiftly on its heels.

With my eyelids drifting shut, I snuggled deeper into his embrace. "I've never spent the night with a man. You're the first."

"Is that right?" His fingertips made lazy circles around my breasts. "Well, I'll have to make sure I'm the last."

CHAPTER 30

ROURKE

*I*n the morning, I awoke to an empty bed but tried not to read anything into it. Roman slept little and worked a lot. We had a busy day ahead of us. The plane for Edinburgh left this evening. I had a million things to do and only a few hours to do them. Of course he was up and going before me.

I dressed in a pair of black slacks and a gray blouse, conservative but sexy. My hair floated around my shoulders to hide the bite marks on my neck. During the trek down the hallway to Roman's study, my stylish black pumps barely touched the ground. Each step brought with it the delicious ache of being rode hard by a skillful lover. *Lover.* Roman Menshikov was my lover. Heat settled in my cheeks. Somehow, in the space of twenty-four hours, I'd gone from devastated to euphoric.

He met me at the door and placed a cup of coffee in my hands. "Good morning, Ms. Donahue."

"Good morning, Mr. Menshikov." The sight of his broad shoulders, draped in navy Armani, sent my pulse into overdrive. "You know how to make coffee?"

"Of course not. I pay people for that." He smiled down at me. "We've got a big day ahead of us. Are you ready for Scotland?"

"Yes. Are you?"

The brush of his lips against my ear made my nipples tighten. We'd had sex three times last night, but it hadn't curbed my need for him in the least. "I'm ready for more of you." Desire flickered in the depths of his blue irises. He dragged a fingertip down the slope of my nose. "But business first. I'll be working from home today. Call the office and let them know, would you? And I've asked Julie to meet with us at eleven."

The phone rang, and the routine of our day began, leaving no time for questions. While he tied up loose ends before his trip, I packed his suitcases and confirmed our flight and reservations.

At five minutes before eleven, I headed downstairs. I had no idea why he wanted to meet with Julie, but as the time for our meeting approached, I grew more and more nervous. Did he think our relationship would interfere with my work performance?

Julie arrived promptly at eleven and took a seat next to me, across from Roman's desk. She gave me a polite nod in greeting, but the tightness of her smile set my nerves alight. I fidgeted in the chair, shifting back and forth, until Roman frowned at me.

"I've asked Julie here today to discuss a change in the terms of your employment." The resonance of his voice soothed my anxiety, although his stern expression didn't help at all. His attention shifted to her. "Julie, Rourke and I have decided to embark on a personal relationship. I need to ensure that she's protected from any backlash by the other employees. Also, I'd like to have the terms of her employment contract revised to her satisfaction."

"Okay." Julie didn't look at me or give any indication of surprise, just nodded in affirmation. "I can make that happen."

"And double her salary."

My jaw dropped. "No. Roman, that's insane. You can't—"

"I already did." He leaned back, smirking at me. "Is there anything else?"

During the course of his speech, my palms had begun to sweat. "No. I don't think so." I licked my lips and cleared my throat. "Except...are you sure about this?" He cocked his head, dark eyes assessing me. "I don't want people to think I'm getting paid to sleep with you."

"I don't care what other people think, and neither should you. Lots of people work together and have a relationship outside of the office. As long as we're upfront about the situation, there aren't any clauses in the company handbook preventing us from seeing each other."

"Yes, that's right." Julie nodded, but her voice carried an odd quaver. Her fingers gripped the arms of her chair, knuckles white. "Technically, you're not an employee of the corporation, so the parameters of her job exist outside of the company structure. I'll make sure the situation is handled with the utmost discretion."

"I appreciate that." Roman's expression remained somber, but the corners of his eyes crinkled. "That's all. We'll see you when we get back from Edinburgh."

I shifted to stand, but Julie remained in her chair. The color drained from her face. "Um, if you don't mind. There's something I need to speak with you about."

A knock rattled the study door. I opened the door. Ivan lurked in the hallway. "May I come in?"

"We were just finishing up here," Roman said.

"Actually, Ms. Baker and I need to speak with you," he said. "It's a matter of some importance."

"Okay. Sure. What can I help you with? Is something wrong?" Roman settled back in his chair and narrowed his eyes at his two closest employees.

"I'm going to go finish up a few things," I said, intending to leave, but Ivan stopped me with a light touch to my shoulder.

"Please stay, if you don't mind."

Something in the tone of his voice made me hesitate. He'd always been quiet and authoritative, but a hint of insecurity ghosted his posture. I closed the door behind him and crossed my arms over my chest.

"Well, spit it out, Ivan," Roman said. "You've got my curiosity going."

Ivan swallowed hard before taking a stance behind Julie's chair. "Ms. Baker and I—Julie—we're going to have a baby."

Silence blanketed the room. I bit the inside of my cheek, my gaze bouncing between the odd couple and back to Roman several times before I overcame the shock.

Roman steepled his fingers over the desk and stared at the pair for a long moment. Finally, he lifted an eyebrow. "Ivan, you sly devil." A slow grin illuminated his face. "Congratulations."

"Julie, I'm so happy for you." I dropped an arm around her shoulders and squeezed. She flinched then turned a deep shade of scarlet. "When are you due?"

"February." With shaking hands, she pushed the hair away from her face. "I'd like to work as long as I can before taking leave."

Ivan stepped forward and rested a hand on her shoulder. The gentleness of his touch brought the sting of tears to my eyes. "We'd like to move in together, if you don't mind. It'll take some accommodation. My apartment is too small for her and the child both."

"Absolutely. Anything you need." Roman stood and pulled

him into a hug. The smile on his face warmed my heart. He rarely smiled and never to this degree, but his genuine happiness for his friend and chief of security spoke volumes about his capacity for caring. "I'm thrilled for you, old friend."

❦

*L*ater that evening, we boarded Roman's private jet for the overnight flight to Edinburgh. I'd never experienced such luxury. Four beautiful flight attendants met us at the cabin door, wearing smiles and matching blue uniforms. The jet's interior echoed the opulence of his penthouse. White carpet and black leather furnishings stretched from wall to wall. A dining table for eight and a master suite with king-size bed topped the list of extravagances.

Roman led me straight to the bedroom after takeoff. Ivan and two security men claimed seats behind the cockpit. As soon as the door shut behind us, Roman began to undress. I sat on the edge of the bed, fingers gripping the soft coverlet, and watched him strip out of his shirt.

"We've got to talk about Nicky," he said without preamble. "There are things you should know about us before we can go further with this relationship."

"You brought me to your bedroom to talk about Nicky?" I asked, trying to grasp the direction of the conversation.

"Our bedroom," he corrected and paused long enough to drop a kiss on my forehead. "First, we talk, and then I'm going to ride you within an inch of your life."

"Oh." A heated blush crawled up my neck. "Get on with it then." I started to unbutton my blouse, but he stopped me with a shake of his head.

"No. I'll do that. You just sit there."

"You certainly are bossy," I said, feeling lightheaded from

the combination of altitude, his cologne, and the sight of his rippled abdomen.

He shook his head, but one corner of his mouth twitched in amusement. "Anyway, as I was about to say before you rudely interrupted me, Nicky and I have a difficult history. When I was eighteen, I went off to Yale, and I met a girl there, Claudette. She was beautiful and smart and from a good family." At his praise, a twinge of possessiveness tweaked my composure. He smirked. "Ah, there's that jealousy. We're going to have to work on that."

"Is there a point to this conversation?" I asked irritably.

"Yes." Deft fingers unbuckled his belt, the button of his trousers, and slid down the zipper. "I fell head over heels in lust with her, and a month later she told me she was pregnant."

"I don't like this story."

"Don't worry. It gets better." His trousers fell to the floor. He stepped out of them and kicked them aside. "I asked her to marry me and invited Nicky over to meet her. They hit it off immediately, which I thought was great." The mattress shifted as he sat beside me. "I wanted to get married right away, but she kept dragging her feet, making up excuses. I tried to blame it on pregnancy hormones and the stress of planning a wedding, but deep down I knew it was more than that. We finally set a date, and a few days before the wedding, she came to me in a mess of tears and confessed that she'd fallen in love with Nicky. They'd been seeing each other on the side, behind my back, for weeks."

"How awful." I slid my hand into his and squeezed. The constant power play between the two men suddenly made sense. No wonder Roman had been incensed over Nicky's mischief.

"You can imagine how angry I was. There's nothing I hate

more than betrayal, especially from the people closest to me. Back then, I had a terrible temper."

"Back then?" I snorted, summoning a chuckle from him.

"Believe it or not, I've mellowed over the years." I rolled my eyes. He flicked open the top button of my blouse, his gaze setting sparks to my desire, and pressed a kiss above the notch of my collarbone. "I threw a fit and cut both of them out of my life. Except for the baby." His eyes softened. "Milada arrived a few months later, and she was the love of my life. We arranged shared custody of her. Eventually, Claudette saw Nicky for who he really is, and she came crawling back to me, saying she'd made a mistake and still wanted to marry me."

"But you said no, right?" I shifted toward him, entranced by the story, wanting to hear more about the mystery of his past.

"I said *hell* no." He smiled and flicked open another button. "I set up a reasonable support payment for Milada and made sure she had everything she wanted, but it just wasn't enough for Claudette. My rejection had wounded her pride. And Nicky never got over the way she came running back to me. Ever since then, he's made it his life's mission to steal any woman I might show an interest in."

I took his hand from my breast and pressed it against my cheek. "I'm sorry about the way they treated you. Not all women are like that, you know?"

He drew my hand to his lips. "I know."

"So now Claudette is punishing you by hiding Milada?" I'd never understood the way parents used their children as instruments of torture against their exes. Claudette rose to the top of my shit list. If I ever met her in person, I'd have a few choice words for her. "Do you have a picture of her—of Milada, I mean?"

"Sure." He grabbed his phone from the nightstand and scrolled through the photos with his thumb. "Here she is. My angel." The first picture showed a naked infant in Roman's lap. He was young and smiling, his face unlined but still handsome. "This one was on her seventh birthday. I bought her a pony." I watched the light grow brighter in his eyes as he flicked from one picture to the next, telling small anecdotes about his daughter. It was the last photograph that made my breath catch. A close up showed Milada as a pre-teen with a wide smile, light brown hair and stunning gray eyes—Nicky's eyes.

"She's beautiful." I bit my lower lip, holding back the obvious retort.

"Yes, she's gorgeous and self-centered and spoiled rotten, but I love her to the ends of the earth and back." With a heavy sigh, he powered off the phone and set it on the nightstand. He took my chin between his thumb and forefinger and tilted my face to his. Dark blue eyes searched mine until I wanted to squirm. "She may not be mine by blood, but she's my daughter in every other way."

My respect for him grew a thousand-fold in that moment. The resemblance between Milada and Nicky was undeniable. Anyone with a pair of eyes could see the truth, yet Roman accepted her as his own, without question.

"Does Nicky know?" I asked when I finally found my voice.

He shrugged, his gaze shuttering for a brief moment. "How could he not? But Nicky doesn't care about anyone other than himself. And he knows I'll be a better father to her than he ever could."

CHAPTER 31

ROURKE

hile Roman attended his meetings, I took the opportunity to explore Edinburgh. I quickly fell in love with the convoluted streets of the old city, the stunning architecture, and its air of mystery. My legs ached from climbing the steps and exploring the length of the Royal Mile. Eventually, I found a bench in the Prince's Street Garden and took a minute to rest.

In the shadows of the Ferris wheel and the Sir Walter Scott monument, everything hit me at once. Aunt May's deterioration. Nicky's betrayal. The absence of my dearest friend. The back-and-forth with Roman. A strangled sob escaped. I clapped a hand over my mouth. Even though I was happier than I'd ever been, it was too much, too fast.

A strand of hair blew over my eyes. I brushed it away and blinked at the appearance of my Prince Charming. Roman strode toward me, shouldering his way through the crowd, looking strong and untouchable. The wind ruffled the lapels of his suit jacket. His long legs ate up the distance between us. Suddenly, I couldn't stand another minute away from him. I sprinted toward him. He caught me in his arms and held me to him, like he never wanted to let go.

"What's wrong?" he asked as he massaged the length of my spine. "You're shaking."

"Just hold me. Please." I burrowed deeper into his embrace. If only I could make this moment last forever.

"Okay." The tip of his nose nuzzled through my hair and along the curve of my ear. "Is it me? Did I do something wrong?"

"No. It's not you. You're perfect. It's me." The more I held him, the harder it was to let go. "I never said I love you, but I do. I love you."

His lips curved into a smile against my neck. "I love you more."

"Wait." I pulled away, searching his face. "What are you doing here? Your meeting isn't over for another hour."

"They found her," he said. The joy and excitement on his face made me forget my worries, because nothing meant more than his happiness. "Milada. Ivan took the jet to get her. They'll be back tonight."

❦

When the door opened on the jet, I had no idea what to expect. Roman stood next to me, his fingers threaded through mine, our sweaty palms pressed together. He pursed his lips and let out a long exhale. Ivan appeared at the door, tall and imposing.

Two seconds later, the round face of a young girl appeared through the opening. She sprinted down the steps and raced toward us. Her long brown ponytail blew in the wind. "Daddy!"

Roman let go of my hand just in time to catch her in his arms. She wrapped her legs around his waist. I backed away, not wanting to intrude on their moment, and blinked back tears. This display of unguarded emotion added a new and unexpected layer to his convoluted personality. My perception of him constantly changed. It would take a lifetime to figure him out, but it was a sacrifice I was willing to make.

"Baby girl, let me look at you." He clasped her face between his large hands and inventoried every inch of her from head to toe. "Are you okay?"

"Yes, Dad. I'm fine." With an exasperated roll of her eyes, she wriggled out of his grasp.

"I missed you so much." He enveloped her in his arms once more, despite her protests.

Over Milada's shoulder, a tall, shapely woman stepped out of the plane. The tails of her white scarf fluttered over her shoulders. Dark sunglasses hid her eyes. A sleek blond chignon framed an oval face, high cheekbones, and full lips. I ran a self-conscious hand over my windswept waves, wishing I'd taken a few extra moments to tidy up before arriving. She strode toward us on sky-high heels, a trench coat draped over her arm.

"Well, Roman, I hope you're happy with yourself. You ruined a perfectly wonderful vacation." Her husky voice carried a hint of French accent. She thrust her coat and purse into my hands. Roman took them from me and shoved them back at her.

"Claudette, Milada, this is Rourke, my girlfriend." As he spoke, he tugged me into his side.

"Hi." Milada turned shining gray eyes to mine. For the second time, I was struck by the similarity between her and Nicky.

"It's nice to meet you both." I smiled at Milada and offered my hand to her mother. Her grasp was cool and hesitant.

"I'm so sorry. I thought you were an employee." Claudette's gaze ran up and down my figure.

I stood up straighter and lifted my chin.

"She's also my personal assistant," Roman said.

Her laugh rang across the tarmac. "Dipping your pen in the company ink. Priceless."

"Actually, it's not," I said, finding my voice again. "He's a perfect gentleman."

"To you maybe." With a toss of her hair, she turned up the wattage on her smile. "So, where are we off to?"

"The three of us are going back to the hotel," Roman said. "I have no idea where you're going. Ivan will get you a cab to your destination."

"You can't be serious." The smile slipped off her face. She wasn't nearly as pretty with her forehead puckered and lips drawn into a sneer.

"But I am." He draped an arm around Milada's shoulders and another around my waist. "Have your lawyer give my lawyer a call. Whenever you're ready to be reasonable, I'm happy to talk."

I'd booked a three-bedroom suite at the Waldorf Astoria because Roman liked to have a lot of space around him, and a separate, smaller room for myself. Ivan and the rest of the security had rooms a few doors away. We hadn't discussed staying together, and I hadn't wanted to press the matter.

"That's hardly fair," I said, dropping a hand to his forearm. "Let me call and see if I can get her a room."

"Do you think it was fair for her to take our daughter out of the country for four months without a word to anyone?" He kept his voice low, directing his words away from Milada. "I don't owe her anything."

"Look, I know you're angry at her, but she *is* Milada's mother. Do you really want her wandering the city at night, looking for a room?"

His shoulders rose and fell with an exasperated breath. "Fine. You're right. She can stay in your room, and you can stay with me." With a light fingertip, he caressed the curve of my cheek. "This is why I need you around. To keep me honest."

"It's turning out to be a full-time job." I tried to keep my tone reproachful, but I couldn't hold back a smile.

CHAPTER 32

ROMAN

*T*hat night, I tucked Milada into bed, despite her protests that she was too old for such nonsense. As she chattered about the places she'd seen during her travels, I marveled at all the ways she'd grown in such a short time. Pretty soon, she'd be thinking about boys and dating. The thought drove me to the brink of madness. How could I possibly protect her from all the dangers of the world when I couldn't even keep her in the same country?

The ache in my chest continued to grow as I turned out the light and made my way back to the master bedroom, where Rourke waited for me. Before Milada had been born, I had no idea that love could be so all-consuming. Now, with Rourke, I'd been exposed to a new and different kind of love. She smiled at me from the bathroom sink, a toothbrush in her hand. A pair of cotton drawstring pajamas hung low on her hips, the ones patterned with pigs, and fuzzy red socks covered her feet.

I closed the bedroom door behind me and went straight to her, because I couldn't wait one more minute to hold her in my arms.

"What are you doing?" she protested through a mouthful of toothpaste.

"I'm taking you to bed, young lady." In one motion, I scooped her off her feet.

"Wait. I need to rinse." I dipped her so she could grab the water glass and finish. "Okay. Take me to bed, Mr. Menshikov."

"That's Prince Menshikov to you." We smiled at each other. I dropped her on the mattress, enjoying the way she threw her head back and laughed.

"How's Milada?" She propped up on her elbows and watched as I shrugged out of my clothes.

"Fine." I couldn't hold back the grin as I spoke about my little treasure. "She was out before I shut off the lights."

"I can't wait to get to know her," Rourke said. "She seems like a sweet girl."

"You'll have plenty of time for that. I'll make sure of it," I said, claiming my place beside her. I nuzzled my nose into her hair, drawing in a lungful of her floral shampoo, and placed a hand on her belly. She was soft and warm and felt like home. I turned onto my side and drew her closer. "When we get back to New York City, I'll have your things moved into my room."

"Excuse me?" With a hand on my sternum, she pushed me away, eyebrows rising. "Just like that? Did you ever think about asking?"

I pretended to ponder for a moment then smiled. "No."

She gave a playful shove to my chest. "Maybe I don't want to live with you." Even though her face was serious, I could tell from the rapid rise and fall of her breasts that the idea excited her.

"Rourke, would you please move in with me?" Her gaze dipped to my mouth. By the way her pupils dilated, I knew I had her. "Let me take care of you. I want to wake up to your smiling face every morning and fall asleep with you in my arms every night."

"Well, since you asked." The brush of her lips over mine caused a stirring between my legs. "Yes." I started to speak but she pressed a fingertip to my mouth. "But you have to stop being so bossy."

I snorted. "We both know that'll never happen." She bit her lower lip to hide her smile, but her eyes shone with amusement. "I'm going to be an arrogant ass, and you're going to get angry with me, and we're probably going to fight each other on a daily basis. But I promise that making up will always be the best part."

"I can't wait." Her arms encircled my neck. I shifted my weight onto her, parting her legs with my knees. Our lips met. The slide of her tongue against mine chased away the worries of the day, thoughts of business, and custody battles.

"You're wearing too many clothes." I slipped a hand inside the waistband of her pajamas. The velvety softness of her skin against my palm made me groan.

"You don't like my pig pajamas?"

"I'd like them better if they were on the floor," I said and turned out the lights.

CHAPTER 33

ROURKE

*T*wo weeks later, I waved to Everly as she cleared immigration at the airport. For someone who'd just traveled halfway around the world, she looked remarkably pulled together in loose-fitting taupe pants and a black sweater. I took her carry-on and handed it to my bodyguard. Everly lifted an eyebrow.

"I'll explain later. Come here. Give me a hug."

We both squealed. She threw her arms around my neck and stamped her feet in an excited dance. "Let me look at you." She held me at arm's length and ran a critical eye over my outfit. "Your hair has grown a mile, and you've lost a few pounds, but something else is different. Something I can't put my finger on." After making a circle around me, she lifted an eyebrow. "You've got a glow. If I had to guess, I'd say someone is putting it to you on a regular basis."

"Everly." I glanced around, hoping no one had overhead.

"Am I right? Who is it?" She hooked an arm through my elbow as we walked toward the baggage claim.

"You can't know that just by looking at me."

"Ha! It's true then." Her step lightened. "I want to hear all about it. Every detail."

"I promise to tell you everything when we get to the car."

At the sight of the long, sleek white limousine, she let out a low whistle. "Gee, you really are happy to see me, aren't you?"

"It's Roman's. He insisted."

Jose greeted us with a tip of his hat and opened the car door.

Once the door shut, a cocoon of silence enveloped us. Everly ran a hand over the fine leather upholstery, tracing the stitching with a fingertip. "Roman, huh? So you guys are on a first-name basis now?"

"Yes, you could say that." Despite my best efforts, I couldn't hold back an ear-to-ear grin.

"No. No way. Rourke Donahue, you spill it right now. I want details, and fast." She tossed her purse aside and slid across the seat to my side.

"He asked me to move in with him, and I said yes." A rush of heat burned my cheeks as I thought of my clothes in his enormous closet, the way he'd made love to me this morning in his king-size bed, and the way it felt to fall asleep in his arms at night.

She stared at me, her mouth opening and closing several times before she found her voice. "You're living with Roman Menshikov, the billionaire prince." A slow grin crossed her face. "Oh, sweetie, I'm so happy. It's all I ever wanted for you."

When we entered the penthouse, I took her upstairs to her room so she could get settled. Roman greeted us in the hall outside her door. He wore dark jeans and a cream sweater with the sleeves pushed up to his elbows. He shook hands with Everly then encircled my waist with an arm and pulled me in for a kiss. I felt her gaze on us.

"Rourke has been over the moon about your visit, Everly. Please make yourself at home," he said.

"Thanks for having me." She turned in a circle, taking in the soaring wall of windows, the splashes of artwork, and graceful architecture. "Are you sure I'm not in the way? I can stay at a hotel. It's not a problem."

"Absolutely not," Roman said. "You girls can have the run of the place, and it'll give me a chance to get to know you better." He gave my bottom a squeeze and my lips a light kiss. "Now, if you'll excuse me, I'm going back to work. I'll see you later."

I watched him go, my attention mesmerized by the lazy grace of his stride. When I turned around, Everly's laughter made my cheeks blush. "What?"

"You guys are cute." Her laughter turned into a choked sob. She sank onto the edge of the bed and dropped her face into her hands.

"Everly, what is it? What's wrong?" I drew her into my arms and rubbed her back until she recovered enough to speak.

"It's my marriage. It's over. I'm not going back." With the back of her hand, she swiped at the wetness on her face. "My husband has a mistress. It's been going on for years. They had a baby together last year." Her sobs redoubled. "I had no idea. I'm such an idiot."

"No, no you're not. He's a bastard." Rage thundered in my ears. The intensity of her tears shook her shoulders. I smoothed a hand down her back, rocking her like a small child. "I'm so sorry. What a fucker."

"Now that I know, there were so many signs. Little things, like all the sudden business trips and the secretive phone calls and the way he'd have to 'run out' for a minute then be gone for hours." I handed her a tissue. She twisted it into a tight knot. "He says he doesn't love her, that it doesn't mean anything, but they have a baby, Rourke. A little girl."

I didn't know what to do or how to make it better. Seeing her pain made my chest ache. She was such a good person; she didn't deserve that kind of treatment. "Do you still love him?"

"How could I love someone who doesn't claim his own child?" Redness rimmed her eyes, but the tears had dried. She sniffed two more times and straightened. "Some things can't be overlooked."

Later that night, after she'd settled in, I crept down to Roman's study and found him pouring over a stack of reports. Milada sat on the floor in front of the fireplace, reading a book. I stood in the shadows and watched them. Every now and then he looked up from his work, to check on her. I knew then that I couldn't live without him. He loved another man's child as his own. He'd taken her in, no questions asked, and never regretted it. I only saw one future for myself, and it was with him.

"Hey, you." A smile brightened his face when he saw me. He'd been smiling a lot more lately, and I liked to think I had a little to do with it. "Come here."

"I don't want to interrupt," I said, but I inched toward him, pulled by an inexplicable magnetism.

He patted his knee, inviting me to take a seat on his lap. I wrapped my arms around his neck and brushed my lips over his. His fingers tightened on my back. When his tongue teased mine, I let out a sigh of contentment.

From a distance, I heard Milada groan. "If you guys are going to make out, I'm going to my room."

Roman pulled back long enough for us both to say, "Goodnight."

We kissed for a long time. The strength in his arms, the heat of his body, and his quiet groans made my panties dampen. I held his face between my hands, enjoying the scratch of his stubble against my palms.

In the background, the fire crackled and popped, casting shadows over the wood paneling. The dancing flames reminded me of the night we'd met at the masquerade. I'd had no idea that a reckless encounter with a mysterious prince would lead to the love of my life.

My thoughts turned to Everly, and I sighed. Her Prince Charming had turned into a toad.

"Is everything okay?" he asked, shifting my weight on his thighs and running a finger along the line of my jaw.

"Yes and no."

His brow furrowed. "Can I help? Name your pleasure, and I'll make it happen."

"It's Everly. She left her husband." Saying the words made my eyes water. When she hurt, I hurt, too. "He's a cheating bastard."

"Lots of men are." His embrace tightened around me. I relaxed into his chest. The rumble of his voice reverberated through his chest and into my back. "You won't have to worry about that with me—not now, and not when we get married."

"Is that so?" My belly gave an excited flip at the mention of marriage. "You sound awfully confident. How do you know I'll say yes?" I toyed with the fabric of his sleeve, watching him through the veil of my eyelashes.

"Oh, you will." The hue of his eyes darkened with a mysterious sparkle. "I'm going to get down on one knee, and I'm going to offer you the biggest, most extravagant diamond I can find."

"So, you're pulling out all the stops for this." Our smiles grew brighter.

"Absolutely. Maybe I'll do it someplace like Bora Bora or Fiji or beneath the Eiffel Tower." His gaze dipped to my mouth and held for the space of two heartbeats. "Or maybe I'll do it right here." Something cool and hard brushed my hand. I glanced down to see the flash of gold and the wink of a princess-cut diamond. One of his eyebrows lifted. "What do you say, Cinderella? Want to be my princess?"

Since I met him, I'd been riding an emotional roller-coaster. My life had gone from boring to action-packed, and I loved every minute of the intrigue, the fighting, and the kisses afterward. I blinked back the tears but they clung to my lashes. "Yes. I'd be honored."

He slid the ring onto my finger. The diamond spanned the entire lower third of my finger. "If you don't like this one, you can pick out something different. Anyone you want."

"It's enormous," I said, overwhelmed by the sight of him, staring up at me with his long-lashed blue eyes reflecting the fire light.

"Like my love for you." Suddenly, he pulled me close, squeezing until my breath ran short. "I need you, Rourke. You're the best thing that ever happened to me. I promise to make you happy or die trying."

"I'm already happy." The damn tears started up again. I dabbed at my cheeks.

"Don't cry, princess. We've got a lot of years ahead of us." He folded my hand into his and kissed the ring.

"I know." I smiled back at him and drank in every line and angle of his face, seeing him through the haze of tears. "And I can't wait to see what happens next."

❦

Thank you for reading The Exiled Prince, Book 1 of the Royal Secrets Series. I hope you enjoy this sneak peek of The Dirty Princess, Book 2.

THE DIRTY PRINCESS

ROURKE

On the day following my marriage to the exiled prince, Roman Menshikov, I awoke in a bed adorned with silk sheets and fluffy down pillows but no prince. The golden February sunrise glowed behind the heavy velvet drapes of our Park Place penthouse. To celebrate our nuptials, we'd slept an extra hour, something Roman never did. I wrapped the top sheet around my naked body, wincing at the soreness between my legs, and tiptoed into the adjoining bathroom. My new husband stood in front of the sink, straight razor in hand, shirtless. Stripes of white shaving cream covered his square jaw and contrasted with the bronze of his skin. I paused to take in the sight of him, imposing, impossibly male, and all mine.

"Good morning, Mrs. Menshikov." The smooth vibration of his voice made my heart skip a beat. His eyes met mine in the mirror.

"Good morning." I hovered in the doorway. Shyness overtook my usual confidence. We'd been living together for a few months before our marriage, first as employer and employee then as a couple. With my thumb, I twirled the band on the third finger of my left hand. *Mrs. Menshikov.* The title made my heart palpitate.

"Did you sleep well?" His gaze went back to his reflection. He scraped the razor along the flat plane of his cheek.

"I didn't sleep at all. You kept me up all night, remember?" The sheet slipped to reveal the top of my breasts. I hitched it higher. His mouth twitched in the smuggest of grins.

"If I didn't have a meeting this morning, I'd have you flat on your back with your legs in the air for the rest of the day," he said. As he spoke, his gaze drifted over my body. The blue of his eyes darkened to navy. There was no mistaking the direction of his thoughts. I loved his desire for me almost as much as I loved his brooding, arrogant sweetness.

"You can have me any way you want me for the rest of our lives." My confidence began to return under his heated stare. I let the sheet whisper to the floor and stood naked in front of him.

"Don't tempt me." In a heartbeat, he wrapped one arm around my waist and took a handful of my rear end with the other. My breasts flattened against his hard pectorals. The wiry hairs on his chest tickled my bare skin. He glanced at his watch. "I have ten minutes. Maybe I should bend you over this counter and—" My knees went weak at the thought. The household intercom buzzed, interrupting his sentence. With a growl, he pressed the speaker button, keeping one hand on my bottom. "What?"

"Mr. Menshikov, your car is ready."

"I'll be down in five." Roman released my posterior and put distance between us, snapping into business mode. I still hadn't grown used to his abrupt mood swings, but he no longer frightened me the way he had in the beginning. He dropped a kiss on my lips, his gaze softening for the briefest of moments. "Don't forget we're meeting with the party planner at three."

"I won't forget." Excitement fizzed in my belly. I retrieved the sheet and draped it around my shoulders like a toga. Roman had decided to let me take over the final arrangements for the Masquerade de Marquis. We'd met at the event last year, and it was one of high society's most coveted gatherings. "When have I ever forgotten one of your appointments?"

"There's always a first time." His wicked grin tore my

thoughts from the masquerade and back to him. I followed him into his dressing room.

"Have I told you lately that you're an overbearing control freak?" While I spoke, I removed his pristine white shirt from the hanger and helped him slide it on.

"Not today, but I'm sure you'll get around to it." The cocky smirk on his handsome face did crazy things to my insides. He buttoned up the front and fastened his cufflinks as I retrieved his tie. His dark head bent to watch as I knotted the length of ice blue silk. "I know we're busy this week, but I've asked Julie to set up interviews right away."

"For what?" I held up his navy suit jacket. Once he'd slid his arms into the sleeves, I smoothed the fabric over his broad shoulders, admiring the V of his torso. No man wore a suit like Roman Menshikov.

"For your replacement," he said.

My fingers halted. We'd gone to city hall on a whim, at his urging. His impromptu request had swept me off my feet, and I'd happily agreed. Neither of us had discussed the particulars of our future beyond generalities. Hearing his request brought the heat of anger to simmer in my veins. "You're firing me?"

"Of course not." Turning his back, he strode into the bedroom. I trotted on his heels, tripping over the long bedsheet. "My wife can't be my personal assistant."

"Why not?"

"Because I said so. You're the wife of a billionaire. You don't need to work." As he spoke, he slipped his phone into the inside pocket of his jacket then gave his reflection a final check in the mirror beside the door.

"Now you're just pissing me off," I snapped. "No one is better qualified to take care of you than your wife. Nothing has changed, Roman." Panic shook my hands. Work meant everything to me.

"Ah, but that's where you're wrong. Everything has changed. You're Mrs. Menshikov now." When I crossed my arms over my chest, he paused to study me. "Are we having our first fight?"

"Yes. We are. We need to talk about this."

"And we will. This evening." He opened the door, signaling the end of our conversation. "Right now, I've got to get to the other side of the city. Where's my briefcase?"

"It's downstairs by the door where it always is." My bare feet slapped on the hall floor. "Roman, you're not seriously leaving?"

At the top of the stairs, he took my chin in his hand. His gaze trapped mine, sending a shiver of need into my center. The tone of his voice gentled. "Later, Rourke."

❀

I hope you enjoyed this sneak peek at the next book in the series. You won't believe what happens next! One-click today.

The Dirty Princess

ALSO BY JEANA E MANN

Felony Romance Series

Intoxicated

Unexpected

Vindicated

Impulsive

Drift

Committed

Pretty Broken Series

Pretty Broken Girl

Pretty Filthy Lies

Pretty Dirty Secrets

Pretty Wild Thing

Pretty Broken Promises

Pretty Broken Dreams

Pretty Broken Baby

Pretty Broken Hearts

Pretty Broken Bastard

Standalones

Monster Love

Short Stories

Everything

Linger

Coming in 2018 - Royal Secrets Series

STAY IN TOUCH

Never miss a new release.

Subscribe to Jeana's newsletter and get the inside scoop on new and upcoming releases, marketing information, FREE BOOKS, sales, book signings, giveaways, and much more!

CLICK HERE

You may unsubscribe at any time. Your information will never be shared without your express permission.

TEXT ALERTS

Text the word "Jeana" (without quotation marks) to 21000 and receive new release alerts straight to your phone.

BEFORE YOU GO

DID YOU ENJOY READING THIS BOOK?
If you did, please help others enjoy it, too.

- **Lend it.**
- **Recommend it.**
- **Review it.**

HELP AN AUTHOR — LEAVE A REVIEW:
If you leave a *positive* review, please send me an email at
jeanamann@yahoo.com or a message on Facebook so that I
can thank you with a personal email.

ABOUT THE AUTHOR

Jeana Mann is the author of sizzling hot contemporary romance. Her debut release *Intoxicated* was a First Place Winner of the 2013 Cleveland Rocks Romance Contest, a finalist in the Carolyn Readers' Choice Awards, and fourth place winner in the International Digital Awards. She is a member of Romance Writers' of America (RWA).

Jeana was born and raised in Indiana where she lives today with her two crazy rat terriers Mildred and Mabel. She graduated from Indiana University with a degree in Speech and Hearing, something totally unrelated to writing. When she's not busy dreaming up steamy romance novels, she loves to travel anywhere and everywhere. Over the years she climbed the ruins of Chichen Iza in Mexico, snorkeled along the shores of Hawaii, driven the track at the Indy 500, sailed around Jamaica, ate gelato on the steps of the Pantheon in Rome, and explored the ancient city of Pompeii. More important than the places she's been are the people she has met along the way.

Be sure to connect with Jeana on Facebook or follow along on Twitter for the latest news regarding her upcoming releases.

Connect with Jeana at
www.jeanaemann.net
jeanamann@yahoo.com

TEXT ALERTS -
text the word "Jeana" without quotation marks to 21000 and
get all the latest marketing news plus new release alerts
straight to your phone.

Copyright © 2018 by Jeana E. Mann

All rights reserved.

No part of this book may be reproduced in any form or by any electronic or
mechanical means, including information storage and retrieval systems,
without written permission from the author, except for the use of brief
quotations in a book review.

This ebook is licensed for your personal enjoyment only. This ebook may not
be resold or given away to other people. If you would like to share this book
with another person, please purchase an additional copy for each person. If
you're reading this book and did not purchase it, or it was not purchased for
your use only, then please return it and purchase your own copy. Thank you
for respecting the hard work of this author. To obtain permission to excerpt
portions of the text, please contact the author at jeanamann@yahoo.com

All characters and events in this book are fiction and figments of the author's
imagination. Any similarity to real persons, alive or deceased, is purely
coincidental.

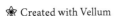 Created with Vellum

CPSIA information can be obtained
at www.ICGtesting.com
Printed in the USA
LVHW011046290820
664259LV00007B/390